Dedication

This book is dedicated to several people who have encouraged me in my pursuit of biblical understanding and application.

First, to my faithful parents, Doug and Marilu Malott, who instilled in me a great love of the scriptures by their example of devotion to reading its inspired words and at the mature ages of 91 and 83 (respectfully) still, pour over its timely message.

Second, to my beautiful and supportive wife Patti, who has encouraged me to read and study the scripture and most recently to write about its majestic beauty.

And third, the wonderful people at the Rock of Ages Christian Fellowship, where I have pastored for many years, who respectfully listen each week to my sermons and teaching and who have inspired me to handle the word of God carefully.

THANK YOU ALL FOR YOUR SUPPORT AND NCOURAGEMENT!

Table of Contents

"The Eye Witness"

Bible Events Described By The People Who Where There!

Douglas S. Malott

THE
HOLY BIBLE,
CONTEINING THE OLD
Testament and the Newe.

Newly Translated out of the Originall Tongues;
and with the former Translations diligently compared
and reuised, by his Maiesties speciall comandement.

Appointed to be read in Churches.

IMPRINTED AT LONDON
By ROBERT BARKER,
Printer to the Kings most
Excellent Maiestie.

ANNO
1613.

Cum Priuilegio.

LEVI SIMEON RVBEN PETER ANDREWE IAMES
IVDAH IOHN
DAN PHILIP
NEPHTHALI BARTHOL
GAD MATTHEWE
ASHER THOMAS
ISSACAR
ZABVLON IOSEPH BENJAMIN MATTHIAS IVDE

TO THE MOST
HIGH AND MIGHTIE
PRINCE, IAMES BY THE GRACE
OF GOD KING OF GREAT BRITAINE,
France and Ireland, Defender of
the Faith, &c.

THE TRANSLATORS OF THE
BIBLE, wish Grace, Mercie, and Peace, through
IESVS CHRIST Our LORD.

REAT and manifold were the blessings (most dread Soueraigne) which Almightie God, the Father of all Mercies, bestowed vpon vs the people of ENGLAND, when first he sent your Maiesties Royall person to rule and raigne ouer vs. For whereas it was the expectation of many, who wished not well vnto our SION, that vpon the setting of that bright Occidentall Starre Queene ELIZABETH of most happie memorie, some thicke and palpable cloudes of darkenesse would so haue ouershadowed this Land, that men should haue bene in doubt which way they were to walke, and that it should hardly be knowen, who was to direct the vnsetled State: the appearance of your MAIESTY, as of the Sunne in his strength, instantly dispelled those supposed and surmised mists, and gaue vnto all that were well affected, exceeding cause of comfort; especially when we beheld the gouernement established in your HIGHNESSE, and your hopefull Seed, by an vndoubted Title, and this also accompanied with Peace and tranquillitie, at home and abroad.

But amongst all our Ioyes, there was no one that more filled our hearts, then the blessed continuance of the Preaching of GODS sacred Word amongst vs, which is that inestimable treasure, which excelleth all the riches of the earth, because the fruit thereof extendeth it selfe, not onely to the time spent in this transitory world, but directeth and disposeth men vnto that Eternall happinesse which is aboue in Heauen.

A 2   The

Acknowledgements

I would first like to thank my family for their support and encouragement in trying such a project as this eBook effort. My wife Patti and all four of my grown children were very positive about the idea, even though it seemed like a lot of work.

Next, I would like to thanks numerous members of my congregation at Rock of Ages Christian Fellowship for their encouragement. Several of the stories were presented as either additions to sermon outlines or dramatically-presented monologues which I read to the church on Sunday mornings. Each presentation was met with very positive feedback and the request for me to consider compiling them in a collection and making them available in published form.

Finally, the finished product could not have been presented without the tedious work of editing. I was fortunate enough to have several talented and available people who patiently read and corrected all of the content: Kudos to Connie Suchomel, Evie Ainley, and Linda Klaja.

Prologue and Introduction

For many of us who love to read the bible, it is more than just biblical history documented on the written page. We believe in its inspired content. It is, for many of us the very word of God conveyed to us through many literary styles and forms. Poetic psalms, prophetic writings, personal letters, historical narrative and other expressions capture the thoughts and words of God from Genesis to Revelation. Each of these forms weaves biblical truth through the lives of countless biblical characters and events and then brings it home to the human heart. In doing so, it attempts to take the *divinely inspired* and make it *humanly applicable*.

As faithful Christians, we all hope to learn from the scripture, find its eternal truth and apply it systematically to our everyday lives. This is as it should be. However, it is my opinion that many times we miss the beauty and drama of the simply described narrative accounts that are found throughout the entire bible. In my mind this is done because of our deliberate concern about finding truth to apply correctly to our daily lives.

Just the Facts Please!

In my view this happens for two basic reasons. The first reason is because we, in our western mindset, opt for a mostly academic approach to scripture study and make it our priority to grasp the 'facts' concerning truth. Thus, we concentrate on finding truth statements, underlining principles, concepts, etc. in the 'wording of scripture'. Again, this is as it should be. We can ill afford to apply scripture based on hearsay, opinions, and possibilities.

All application must begin with the true essence of the written scripture. However, making this our solitary approach seems to me to make the scripture look like a 'black on white' uncolored page in a coloring book. The image is clear, the picture understandable and the basic facts stand out to us, but left without 'color' the page lacks depth and personality.

Biblical Styles of Writing!

The second reason has to do with the way in which the original texts where written. The narrative writers of the old and new testaments were writing to people who understood the culture, the customs and habits of the people involved and so such detail was not always needed in the narrative. Their primary concern was in conveying the main aspects of the event so that a basic history could be preserved. The priority was to describe Gods panoramic plan of salvation as it extended throughout all of the biblical narrative. This meant that much of the personal drama unfolding behind the scenes was not needed, simply not known or minimized to make the main point of the story stand out.

For the most part, events were recorded after the fact from inspired memory and thus information about the thoughts, emotions, opinions, and potential reactions etc. of those involved could not always be recorded, unless of course the writer was involved in the event himself and then made attempts to add additional personal perspective. This approach alone is again like the previously mentioned uncolored page of a coloring book. We see the images, understand the picture but have to supply our own color to give the picture its depth and final completeness.

What is left is the need for the reader to fill in his own color to the page. We are left to imagine the secondary, supportive or background details of the events as they unfold. Our own imagination must at times fill in many of the background details, behind, around and within the bold black lines of the actual biblical text.

In this book, I have simply attempted to take familiar biblical events and describe them from the perspective of a probable 'eye witness'; some who were there but were presented anonymously or some who were there as main characters but nameless in the text. In some cases I invented characters that conceivably would have been there to observe the actual event and then let them describe their experience. The stories I have written are formed from the text of several bible events.

I have attempted to remain true to the original bible text and simply developed a first person narrative of the event from the viewpoint of a bystander, fictitious person or non-descript character in the original story. In this way the bold black lines of the scripture's narrative are preserved with great care. I simply help the reader color in between the lines with believable support narrative. I call this, for my own definition purposes, a **'written dramatic adaptation of the biblical narrative'**.

It is not my intent to teach or instruct, although the characters in the narrative do learn from their experience. Rather I want to bring the text alive with very plausible and realistic dramatic adaptation so the account takes on a more colorful perspective for the reader. In this approach I hope the reader will find an easy to read, enjoyable and perhaps enlightening encounter with the bible and its people.

Originally, several of the stories were written as first person monologues and read dramatically to my congregation in the place of a formal sermon or message. On each of the three occasions where this was done I actually dressed in full replica costumes to recreate a background feel for the story. So, for example, on Christmas Sunday a 'Bethlehem Shepherd' tells the story of the birth of Jesus as he would have experienced it. Later, a 'Roman Centurion' retells the account of the 'Triumphal Entry and Crucifixion of Jesus' and finally a 'Garden Tomb Guard' recounts his experience of the resurrection of Jesus. After writing these monologues and compiling several others it seems plausible to attempt a compellation of all of the stories into book form.

For the most part care has been taken to research background information and historical facts and insight to insure that descriptions are true to their time periods and cultural setting. My goal has been to write an enjoyable and easily read account of the bible from the perspective of people we would normally not think about in the narrative.

Each of the accounts is written as a standalone short story allowing the reader to pick and choose individual chapters without the requirement of reading them in sequence. I trust it will be as enjoyable to read as it was to write!

CHAPTER ONE:
BACK FROM THE DEAD
JOHN 11

Historical background and setting

The year was approximately 33 A.D. This was to be the final year of Jesus' life and public ministry. Late in this year He would be arrested and crucified, but before those infamous days arrived Jesus performed one of his most notable miracles. In John chapter 11, we see Jesus travel to Bethany where a close friend has recently died. While there, with his disciples watching, several personal friends grieving and numerous other individuals present, he raises his friend Lazarus from the dead. This was done four full days after his burial in a local tomb.

The town of Bethany is located just a short 2 miles from Jerusalem. Being just an hour's walk from Jerusalem, Israel's capitol city and religious center allowed for quick access to the grieving family of Lazarus. As was the custom, religious leaders, priests and other orthodox Jews would be on the scene of such a loss of life to comfort the surviving loved ones of the deceased. This was the case for Mary,

Martha and others after Lazarus' death and burial. Jesus would arrive in the middle of the public grieving that no doubt was the center of activity for this small village suburb of Jerusalem.

The Story

I am an anonymous character in the biblical narrative. I had the privilege of being a personal friend of both Martha and Mary and thus was committed to being at their side after the death of their brother Lazarus. Expecting to grieve and console my friends, I experienced instead a dramatic introduction to Jesus the Messiah. This is my story.

It is never easy to face the death of a loved one. Even if sickness has drained the life out of the body and death is expected to arrive soon, it is never easy. It is this reality that prompts me and all good Hebrew people to stand ready and be available to those who must endure this kind of loss. The day I heard of Lazarus' passing, brought a strange rush of grief as well as relief, having watched my good friend Martha endure the suffering of her brother for many weeks. Immediately upon hearing the news I made arrangements to travel to Bethany with the hope of being a comforting presence to the entire family.

Martha and I had been friends since childhood. We had grown up together in the small village of Bethany where both of our families worked, played and worshipped together. Our closeness made it possible for us to share many of the same friends and acquaintances and helped us stay in contact over the years. Even after I moved into the city of Jerusalem to work, we continued to see each other and share our lives as much as possible. In recent years I had been concerned with the way Martha and her sister had become so engrossed in the teachings of a certain Jesus of Nazareth, a local holy man and supposed prophet. I was especially agitated about the excessive time they spent hosting him in their home and even traveling with him during his wanderings through our nation. On the occasions that I was able to speak with Martha about my concerns, she would simply encourage me not to be troubled about their activities. Instead, she pressed me to come and listen to this teacher speak of the kingdom of God. To hear her talk, one would think that the kingdom of heaven had come to earth in the form of this man! I, of course, was skeptical and did not think I needed to hear him expound on God's kingdom.

I held my concerns privately, as not to offend my dear friend, but was not ready to surrender my strongly held Hasidic traditions in favor of this itinerate preacher! It was thus no surprise when, upon arriving in Bethany and settling into Martha's home, she informed me of the urgent message she had sent to this Jesus informing him of Lazarus' sickness. It was clear to me that she held some lofty notion that if he had only been there to greet his dear friend Lazarus, somehow the man would not have died. I attributed this wishful thinking to her great love for her brother, not to any clear proof that this Jesus could indeed have done such a thing. As I look back on that time now, I only wish I could have believed just a little in what Martha had told me. I would then not have been so shocked and embarrassed by what I witnessed later as those grieving days progressed and the preacher did arrive…finally…on the scene.

Sadness hung in the air like an invisible veil cloaking every heart and mind. At the slightest word or expression, tears would flow and anguish would be raw and fresh. Family members were gathered in small groups with visiting friends, sharing in each other's grief and attempting to bolster emotions with the good and noble memories of the past. Although food was available, few partook of the hospitality, being in no mood for delicacies at such a time as this. Out of respect for the dead and those who were grieving, the women were dressed in black. Of the few men who were present, most were subdued in both fashion as well as speech. Many filled the simple home and small courtyard that served as a buffer to the main living quarters, although some made their way to the grave site to better express their tears and sorrow. This scene that played out before me would no doubt last the customary seven days, and since it had been just four days since the death and burial of Lazarus an intense atmosphere of sorrow, grief and questioning still enveloped each of us!

In particular, Martha and her sister, Mary, were carrying the heaviest part of this weight as they were the closest to their dear brother. And both questioned the absence of the preacher they respected so deeply, especially since they were certain he could have prevented this tragedy. It seemed to me that their tears were mixed with disappointment and agitation at the apparent dismissal of this Jesus of Nazareth. I caught many short comments and trailing conversations that spilled over with questions, doubts and "what if's". I was certain that each of them was still wrestling with the finality of their brothers' death, attempting every so often to push the thought away in a vain attempt to bring him back to life.

When word came to us that the preacher had been seen approaching the village, there was no small stir in the house. Family members, in particular, became animated and alert although just moments before they had been drowsy and dumb with grief. It was clear to me that the preacher's imminent arrival had sparked something in them…something that seemed to me, at least temporarily, to dispel the mood of hopelessness. Martha rose quickly to her feet and hurried out the front entrance, through the courtyard, and down the rocky pathway that led to the main road. It was there she met this Jesus of Nazareth and the group of disciples who were his constant companions.

As I heard later, Martha had no sooner met and greeted him when the words tumbled from her questioning heart, "Lord, if you had only been here, my brother wouldn't have died. But indeed even now I know that whatever you ask from God, He will give you."

The preacher, I was told, replied to her immediately, 'Your brother will rise again!' attempting to give her a brief glimpse into the future heavenly kingdom, no doubt, in hopes of comforting her grief a little.

Those standing with the group arriving on the road also heard his words. I am quite certain they thought exactly what Martha put into words next: "I know that he will rise again in the resurrection at the last day."

Any sensible person at this juncture would have simply agreed with her final statement and left it at that, hoping to move forward and offer some comforting thoughts that would bring a healthy sense of reality to the conversation. But the preacher did no such thing! Apparently, as all reports have it, he seemed to encourage Martha with the expectation of a resurrection much sooner than on the last day, to which Martha apparently said, "I believe You are the Messiah, the Son of God, who comes into the world." When hearing of this response I made a mental note to talk sternly to my friend as soon as the grieving time had concluded. To me, it was one thing to appreciate the teaching of some new rabbi but quite another to think of him as the Messiah. Little did I know at that precise moment, that I would soon have my own reason for believing him to be the Messiah!

Back in the house where I was sitting with Mary, we could see Martha take leave of the preacher and head directly toward us. As she entered the room, she insisted that Mary greet the preacher since this 'so called messiah' was asking for her by name. Mary rose quickly to her feet, moved through the crowd and the courtyard, and then toward the road. Several people, including myself, jumped to our feet to go with her, assuming that she was going back to the tomb to shed more tears for her brother. When I realized that she was not going to the tomb, but rather to meet the preacher, I was troubled. Was this the best choice? What could this man do now? Perhaps had he come earlier, before Lazarus had passed, maybe he could have encouraged him to rally beyond his illness… but now? It was just too late!

I am not sure what I expected to see when Mary and our group reached the preacher. Perhaps I expected a fiery prophet like Elijah of old, or perhaps a wilder eyed unstable sort that projected mysticism or intrigue. I had only heard stories of this man and most were told to me by those who were suspicious of his message and claims. At the very least, I envisioned an unsavory type with every sort of disqualifying trait imaginable. What I saw was just the opposite. What I saw unsettled me, disarmed me completely, and in a moment dispelled all my suspicious notions. This man carried about himself an air of humility and strength that seemed authentic and real. His face was soft and inviting and his eyes had a beckoning quality to them. There, surrounded by his followers, he was kneeling down with his hand placed gently on Mary's head. She had arrived a few steps before the rest of us and had fallen directly at the preachers' feet in a heap of spent emotion and sorrow. He seemed to be instantly moved by Mary's broken heart, instantly in touch with her grief, and at the same time angered in his spirit by this state of affairs that had induced her desperate sorrow. His eyes were ablaze with compassion and concern as she, too, declared that her brother would not have died had he been there earlier. At this, the preacher seemed to stiffen a bit as if to recoil at his own tardiness! Expecting Mary to gather herself emotionally and beckon the preacher toward the house, and the preacher to gather her to his strong side and guide her back to the rest of the grieving friends, I was taken back by his request to be taken to the tomb. 'Where have you put him?' he questioned urgently.

As the preacher and his disciples were taken to the site of the tomb, the entire household emptied. Everyone wanted to see the famous preacher and watch his reaction, or at the very least to join him in his grieving over his friend. Martha led the crowd from the house and acted as a rally point for all who were winding their way up the lonely barren path to the closed tomb. It was all I could do to keep up with Mary and the preacher as they were led to the gravesite. This Jesus was not to be distracted as he climbed the slight hill to the stone that covered the tomb. It appeared to me that he was walking with purpose and intent as he climbed. He was the first one to arrive, with Martha joining him soon after, followed by Mary. Quickly the mourners, including myself, filtered into the area and silently formed a viewing audience of several dozen. What met our ears as we finally became quiet and stood facing the closed tomb was not silence as one might expect, but the soft and low sounds of crying. The preacher, the teacher, this "so called messiah', was crying visibly and publicly for his friend. At the sight of his tears, many of the mourners were moved by the compassion he displayed. Whispers began drifting through the crowd as people commented about his obvious love for his friend. Some, who evidently were familiar with this man's ministry, wondered out loud if indeed he who had opened a blind man's eyes could have somehow kept this man from dying. I, on the other hand, did not think that his arrival could have changed the course of Lazarus's death.

The preacher soon quieted his soft crying and turned to gaze intently at the tomb. From my vantage point, it appeared that the same anger I had seen earlier flashed in his eyes again –with an intensity that seemed to pierce right through the stone barrier of the tomb. For a disquieting moment, it seemed as if he was considering the contents of that death chamber and actually signaled to it! Could he see into that dark place by some divine power? And if so, what was his intent? It certainly did not appear as though he simply desired to join the grieving parties who were present. Something other than sympathy was now spreading across his face. In a very deliberate motion he turned toward Martha and Mary, but looked more directly into the atmosphere surrounding them. At that moment, he spoke to no one in particular, but his words brought a rise of emotion to the entire crowd. "Remove the stone" he commanded firmly. He made no grandiose gesture or dramatic scene for the sake of the bystanders; he simply issued a directive that the tomb's stone closure be removed.

Martha suddenly responded with great concern. She stated in no uncertain terms that Lazarus had been dead four full days and that exposing his decaying body to the light of day would no doubt produce a great stench. The shock in her voice was unmistakable, as was her fear of disturbing the dead and thereby being unwillingly subjected to the inglorious processes of physical death. Nonetheless, the preacher insisted, "Didn't I tell you that if you believed you would see the glory of God?"

With that, Martha motioned to several men in the crowd. Each of them slowly walked to the tomb. And together, with much labor and struggle, they rolled the stone door away from the mouth of the cave. For a few awkward moments, only the sound of the great stone scraping against the side of the tomb could be heard. As the stone slowly exposed the hollow darkness behind it, a measurable tension penetrated the air. Each of us stared uneasily into the blackness of Lazarus' resting place. Many covered their faces in hopes of preventing the stench of death from reaching them. What could the preacher be thinking? I thought to myself. I could feel the rush of emotion pushing and clawing at my heart, a slight shiver prompted the thought that I wasn't reacting to a perceived chill in the air, but rather to the fact that I could not fathom what it could mean to make such an unthinkable and unreasonable request. Insisting that the tomb be opened? It was almost rude and offensive!

While we were reeling internally at the developing scene, the preacher simply turned his gaze from the open tomb and directed his eyes toward the sky. He seemed to be praying, conversing with God in a way that was so personal and reassuring. He made no effort to conceal his intercession; it was as if he spoke into the air purposely for the sake of us unbelieving and skeptical onlookers. Almost with the same breath, after addressing heaven, he faced the tomb again and shouted with a strong and determined voice, "Lazarus, come out!" For a brief moment his voice echoed and reverberated around us as his words were spoken.

I was stunned. We all were stunned, with perhaps the exception of Mary. I had not expected this preacher to speak to the dead; nor had I, in my wildest thoughts, expected him to address death itself! Yet, he had dared to do so! For a few brief moments, we watched the scene unfolding before us in a suspended state of inertia…reduced to little more than human statues. The dark hole of the open tomb stared back at us. The preacher, having just called to the dead man, was standing at the edge of the crowd expecting something to happen. Mary and Martha, with tear-streaked faces, fixed their hopeful eyes on the tomb in sheer exhilaration. The crowd, silent, wondering and tense, held its corporate breath.

Into the silence of this sober –and almost holy— moment, came the muffled sound of shuffling feet. Gentle, but unmistakable, scraping and scuffling sounds could be heard from the floor of the tomb. Dirt and rock and dust were being pushed and spread by movement. Slowly, in the shadowy brown-grey recesses of the cave, a form began to take shape and emerge. Gasps and cries escaped the lips of the people as they watched in awe, vainly attempting to control their amazement! While the features were not recognizable at first glimpse of the shuffling dead man, there was no doubt in our minds as to whom this might be.

It was Lazarus! The once dead man was alive.

He struggled with the burial material that still bound his hands to his side and kept his feet and ankles scooting along the ground, but he was very much alive. Alive indeed!

His face remained hidden behind the customary burial head covering, and his eyes strained through the thick cloth to make his way out into the light of day without falling. But he was alive. Alive indeed!

No one moved! No one *could* move! The sight of this resurrected man kept us frozen in place. We could not believe our eyes! I, for one, grappled with a hundred thoughts that sped through my head. On the surface of my soul, I told myself that this could not be happening. And yet as I watched this newly revived man struggle forward, deep in my spirit I wanted to shout praise to the God of heaven. Had anything like this ever happened in Israel… at least in our day? I did not think so; and thus my mind was driven directly to this preacher.

Who…was…this…man? What…was…his…purpose? Was Martha correct? Was he indeed the promised Messiah? I suddenly felt as if during these past two years I had been missing the most significant event of our time! I did not know, in this moment, whether or not this preacher was the Messiah, but given what I had just witnessed, it seemed to me that he certainly should be!

My thoughts were abruptly interrupted with the preacher's next orders, "Loose him and let him go." Mary, Martha, friends and family now rushed toward Lazarus. No expense or energy was spared in taking the grave clothes off his body. In an instant he was free, taking in the light of day and being lovingly mobbed by everyone. Even the preacher welcomed him back to life.

Now full of excitement for the family, I pressed myself forward to embrace Lazarus along with most of those who were present. I also felt a keen warmth, acceptance and respect for the preacher. In fact, I began hoping that he was truly the promised Messiah. I truly could not imagine that any who had witnessed this miracle could think otherwise. At the mere command of his voice, a dead man had come to life! The effects of four full days of death and decay had been reversed and cancelled by this simple man from Galilee. But it was not long before I would hear just the opposite. Apparently, even before the once dead man had been able to remove his own grave clothes, some in the crowd had become angry and left the scene ready to give suspicious and negative reports to the Pharisees. In time, we would all know of their evil response.

But, in this moment, what had been a long week of grieving and sorrow was now turned to great celebration and joy! Lazarus, who had been dead, was now very much alive, giving clear testimony to the calling of this Jesus and his messianic purpose!

CHAPTER TWO:
HOPE HAS COME!
THE CHRISTMAS SHEPHERD'S STORY
LUKE 2:8-18.

Historical background and setting

The year is approximately 5 BC. In the small town of Bethlehem, where Mary and Joseph have arrived from a long journey, the birth of Jesus will occur. The Wise men have yet to arrive, which will be about 2 years in the future from this point in time. Herod the Great is in his final years as King of Judah, and will die a horrible death, just a few short years after ordering the massacre of the innocent children of Bethlehem. In the Gospel of Luke's account of the birth of Jesus Christ, Angels will announce the miraculous birth, first, to shepherds watching their sheep in the Judean hill county. It will be these shepherds who will be the first to visit the new born baby. From this setting, one of the shepherds will give us his personal description of what it was like to have been there.

The Story

I am an anonymous shepherd. My whole life was spent tending sheep on the Bethlehem hills. It was there that I had the privilege of being included in the announcement of the birth of the Messiah to the world, and joined my companions in being the first to worship Him in His small manger throne. This is my story.

Have you ever been without hope, felt hopeless, felt like nothing would break your way? Day after day, year after year, mounting unfulfilled dreams and needs staring you in the face, mocking your meager existence? Perhaps you have. I did, we all did. My hopelessness was as personal as it was geographical. You see, I shared a nationwide hopelessness with most of my fellow Jews, in particular, my fellow shepherds. As a proud people with a proud history, we lived with memories and tales of better days; days when our strong Hebrew kings governed us and led our armies. In those past days of glory the Lord Jehovah would speak through His prophets, direct and lead the armies of Israel, and honor our sacrifices by defending us against all of our enemies!

But, in the course of time, those days faded as our obedience faded. We were forced to face a new reality! God had ceased to speak, and in time we turned our back and drifted away from His law, and were eventually obligated to the laws of many conquering nations. Now we lived under the rule of the pagan and idolatress Roman Empire. Hopeless and suffering, we prayed and longed for the Messiah to come. We looked for God's chosen one, His chosen deliverer, to appear and revive us. We yearned for His mercy to forgive His people and restore our national glory.

What actually happened in Bethlehem that night was not what most people were expecting! Oh a few, whose hearts had remained true toward God, embraced His plan, but most were unsuspecting and unprepared. God heard the cries of His people and indeed heard the cry of all humanity.

He set in motion the most incredible and bizarre arrangement to bring His chosen one to Israel and the world. It was so strange and peculiar that only after seeing Him for myself did I come to understand and embrace this new way.

It was only after accepting God's new revelation did the spark of hope spring to life in my heart again. A spark of hope that grows brighter and stronger with each passing day.

I can still remember the events of that night as if they happened yesterday. I was just a young boy of 13 years of age at the time, but the strange and wonderful things that took place on that clear star lit night forever changed the world, my people Israel, and of course me. As a lowly shepherd, I was destined for little in life except tending sheep. My father had done it, and his father's before him so it was hopeless to think of anything else for me. I had not thought anything would make me feel different about my meager future and the shepherding life…until that night. A grand miracle would change my thinking, bring faith alive, and give purpose to my life, all in one long amazing night.

Shepherds are born for the hill country, you know. Rolling, meandering, low hills in the Bethlehem foothills was home to many shepherds. Their whole existence was to care for their family flocks of sheep and goats. A Judean shepherd knew the hill county like the back of his weathered hand. He lived on those craggy outcroppings and prodded his flock as a constant habit from one grazing area to another. If he did not do so, the flocks would suffer through malnourishment, perhaps die or become easy prey for predators. Or at the very least, their lack of adequate food could make them restless, uncooperative, and just plain troublesome. So we, as shepherds, were constantly on the move looking for good grazing, watching for the next water source and green pasture to feed our flocks.

Vigilance, of course, was the name of the game both day and night. We were watching the flocks for stragglers, urging them with rod and staff to stay close and thus stay safe. Our acute alertness involved scanning the vistas and horizon for possible intruders that could attack our flocks. We were guardians; we were protectors as well as family businessmen attempting to make a living in our effort to raise our flocks and get them to market. And with the Temple rituals and sacrificial requirements still heavy upon the whole nation, good, clean, and spotless animals could go at a premium. Especially if King Herod and his officials were buying!

Many of us shepherds were proud of our rich Hebrew heritage. Many times we would recount the stories of our beloved King David of old, and remember that God had called him to be king from his father's sheepfolds. As a young boy I dreamed of defending my father's flock from the lion and the bear like David had done, and perhaps proving myself worthy of being chosen by God again for some great task or assignment. We as God's people so needed a hero, a savior, someone to right the many wrongs that we the Jews had suffered. Such shame, humiliation, and destruction over the centuries had brought Israel to this low point of despair and hopelessness. Redemption, deliverance, salvation seemed a vague notion, an unreachable dream. But in my dreams and prayers I believed that maybe once more God would liberate His people, end their captivity, and restore hope to our proud nation by the hand of another great shepherd leader. Let Jehovah be praised! May He deliver Israel once again! This was my constant prayer.

That night the atmosphere had grown dark with the setting sun and we had spent quite some time gathering sticks and briars and old broken limbs to make our sheepfold for the overnight hours. Some had carried stones and rocks to make a small protective wall for the animals. This was done every night to protect the flock from predators, as we, the shepherds, took turns keeping watch at the door of the fold.

This particular night started like most others as we all settled into our routine for the night. The Bethlehem hills were beautiful and tranquil in the stillness of night. In the distance I could see the flickering, dwindling lights of the town of Bethlehem as its habitants turned to sleep. We had been told that the town was packed with pilgrims from all over Israel who were required to return to the place of their family origin to be counted in the great Roman census. It was at a time like this that I was glad to be far away from the turmoil and frantic congestion of Bethlehem and out here watching my flocks. No doubt, with such a crush of people attempting to gather in Bethlehem to be registered, there would not be a single good place to stay, let alone enough food for all. Shepherding was not a glamorous job, but at times like this it did have its advantages.

Across the valley on the other side of Bethlehem, rising like a shadowy monster in the blackness, stood one of King Herod's palaces', the Herodium. We, as sheep herders, were careful not to get too close to those quarters for fear that somehow we would find ourselves in violation of the King's whim or rage, and suffer greatly for our foolishness. Often, as I would look out over the valley to that regal but terrifying place, I would wonder what privilege or favor or treasures could be found inside those protected kingly walls, especially since much of Judea suffered in poverty and anguish of soul. On this night, it seemed to me, that I could make out distant glinting of light at the windows and gates of the giant fortress. Perhaps Herod was in residence on this most unusual night, if so, it would be a most unusual and prophetic coincidence.

The night sky seemed to me to be particularly clear and endless. Almost as if the whole of the starry host were waiting in anticipation of something grand. As a young boy, the night hours often played games with my mind and imagination. It tended to serve up images of strange creatures or ghostly shadows, bearing some bandit or robber or perhaps a valiant warrior attacking his foe. This night was no different, and as the night deepened, sleep was a welcomed relief from the nervous imaginations in my childish head.

I was just drifting off to sleep, in fact, when the angels first appeared. It seemed instantly as though the night had turned to day again. The brightness was almost blinding. It seemed the whole of the sky was ablaze. Shadows were gone, hiding places were exposed, and I felt that everything was somehow open to heaven's view. But the light wasn't all we saw. In the blazing spread of light there seemed to be hundreds and hundreds of faces, thousands of wings, and voice after voice after voice joining in unison to bring a message. If the blazing light, hovering wings and thundering voices weren't enough, the idea that the announcement was being made to us; simple shepherds in the field; watching over our flocks by night was shocking. It wasn't really until days later that we pondered as to why the announcement wasn't made elsewhere to more important people. But in that moment we simply were overwhelmed and terrified. Any earlier fears brought on by the shadows of nightfall were instantly minimized. I was now quivering and shaking like a tiny oak leaf in a violent wind storm. It seemed heaven had come to earth and decided to show up on our hill side.

We were being confronted and presented with an announcement of celestial proportions.

'Do not be Afraid'... an angel had called to us.

'I bring you good news' ...the angel had said.

'News of great joy for all people' ...he had shouted from the sky.

'A savior has been born, Messiah the Lord' ...the angel proclaimed.

'In the city of David' ...he had said.

'Go look for a sign' ...the angel had prodded.

'A baby wrapped snuggly in cloth' ...he had continued...'lying in a feeding trough'.

And then in one grand choir of sound and light...'Glory to God in the highest and peace on earth to all men', the heavenly host had shouted in one great crescendo, and then concluded.

As the voices of the angels faded, and the heavenly light slowly retreated back into heaven, all that was left was absolute silence. All of us were shocked, astonished and speechless. No one said a word for what seemed like 'forever'. We dared not speak, could not speak. We simply stared into the sky, and then back to each other, as the reality of what had just happened broke over our minds and hearts like a Judean downpour. We were being told that the Messiah was here. Centuries of believing and waiting, and hoping and hoping against hope even, were now, we were being told, at a close. We had been awakened by angels, almost blinded by heavenly light, serenaded by the heavenly host, and all for the purpose of announcing the Messiah. What had begun as an ordinary night on the Judean countryside had ended with a dramatic, spectacular announcement: Israel's hope, my hope, indeed the world's hope, had come.

Eventually, from somewhere in the back of the sheepfold, a quivering voice, struggling to find strength, called out. 'Come, let's go! We must see this thing that the Lord has made known to us. Let's go straight to Bethlehem and find this babe in the feeding trough.' It would normally have seemed a strange thing to do at this time of night, but suddenly, on this night, it was the only thing we could do. So with quick preparation, and a wary eye on half sleeping and stumbling sheep, we began our journey off the hill side and down into the town of Bethlehem.

Bethlehem lay mostly asleep on its cozy hillside when we arrived. No one seemed aware of any special birth event or urgent angelic directive. So upon arriving, several of our party began to inquire of the newly born baby.

Did they know He had been born?

Did they know where He might be staying?

Was anyone aware that this birth was divinely planned?

Angels had awakened us from our sleep on the hill side and told to us to come, could someone direct us to the place of His birth?

Our insistent inquiries eventually yielded the information we needed. Apparently there had been no room for a tired, well traveled, pregnant woman and her husband earlier in the day. Whether the local boarding establishment had no place for them...or...whether their family, out of embarrassment, would not make room available, we could not know. The pregnant mother and anxious father had been directed to the only place available; the local stable. We knew the stable well. Shepherds and their flocks were always directed to the stable, when on their journeys. So we made our way, out some distance beyond the Inn, to the cave-like setting that was designed to house animals and their tenders. It was there that we caught our first glimpse of the baby Messiah.

We found the infant indeed in a feeding trough, and yes, wrapped snuggly in tight warm blanket strips. He was being held securely by his weak but smiling mother and watched over by an admiring father. And this divine and poignant scene was surrounded by straw and dirt, dust, foul odors, beasts of burden, and now stunned but admiring shepherds.

We and our clumsy collection of sheep and goats made our way to this babies' side. Seeing the baby Messiah in this hidden but holy place, brought on a strange mixture of feelings: reverence, giddiness and wonder, were stirred in us all. It was exactly as the angels had announced. We just hadn't expected to find Him in this almost forgotten place. Here in the most unusual and inconspicuous of places, God had sent the Messiah, as a baby. He had not come as a ruling king, or a victorious warrior, nor had he come as a wise man or sage. The hope of the world had come as a baby, announced to shepherds, born and placed in a feed trough. Under the view of heaven, and the blind eye of both Rome and Israel, the Savior was born in Bethlehem.

Well, needless to say, we were overwhelmed. One by one, without human prodding, we bowed and knelt before the baby. I could see the pleased but puzzled look on the parents faces as they watched our humbled actions. It was only right that God's Chosen One be worshipped! What we had seen and heard on the hill side, and then seen and touched in the stable, moved us beyond anything we had ever experienced. As the night slowly turned toward day, and the stirring of our flocks required us to leave the couple and their baby, we made our way back to the hills and out over the Judean country side. As we traveled and prodded our wayward flocks onward, we talked to everyone we encountered. We simply could not be silenced! We told about what we had seen and heard and boldly insisted that hope was alive again. God had sent the Messiah, and soon all would hear and see Him for themselves. A new shepherd leader had indeed arrived. Hope had come! *May the Lord, Jehovah and His Messiah, Jesus be praised forever! Amen!*

DOUGLAS S. MALOTT

CHAPTER THREE:
GARDEN TOMB GUARD
MATTHEW 27:50-28:15

Historical background and setting

     The year is approximately 30 A.D. Jesus Christ had been crucified at the hands of both the Romans and the Jewish leaders. He has been placed in a borrowed tomb in a small garden just outside the city walls of Jerusalem. To insure that His body is not stolen by his disciples or followers, the High Priest and Elders have asked Pontius Pilate for a guard unit to stand guard over the sealed tomb. The disciples are in hiding and are mourning the death of Jesus and all of Jerusalem, indeed all of Israel, is in the process of finishing the annual celebration of the Feast of Passover and beginning the weeklong feast of unleavened bread. In this setting the resurrection takes place, and a most unlikely witness of the event now tells his story.

<u>The Story</u>

I am a Roman soldier in hiding; in self imposed exile! Having been assigned the duty of guarding the sealed tomb of one Jesus of Nazareth, I found myself being a witness to the most provocative event in all of human history; the resurrection of Jesus Christ. From my secure and anonymous place of hiding, well away from the City of Jerusalem, I gather enough inner strength and resolve to write home to my family. Having left with little word or instruction, I now decide to explain my absence, and for the first time since that fateful day, describe my experience in the garden and my new found faith. This is my story.

My dearest family and friends,

I trust this correspondence finds you well, safe and blessed. It is I Tertinius who write these words to you all. I think of you often and fight back tears of grief almost daily as I think of this separation and its prolonged effect on all of us. As my departure from Judea, so many months ago, was sudden and largely unexplained, I am sure your hearts have been crushed with despair wondering what has become of me. Hopefully you are not disturbed by the abrupt arrival of this letter. The memory of the shock and sadness in your eyes, as I informed you of my need to leave, constantly haunts me. But not as much as the images that war in my mind concerning those fateful days of the Jewish Passover and the crucifixion of that man Jesus. His crucifixion at the hand of Rome and the temple leaders began a disconcerting but needed change for me and my mostly empty life.

Upon hearing extraordinary reports coming to my ears from Judea concerning the new sect of disciples, called Christians, I felt I must write to you. These so called Christians, who determine to follow the teachings of Jesus of Nazareth, are increasing in numbers through the whole of the Roman Empire. And many are giving testimony to having experienced this Jesus in some kind of supernatural fashion, since the first reports began to surface concerning

His supposed resurrection. I now know that I will never forget the unearthly happenings that I experienced over those days of the crucifixion, and in particular the glory of that morning in the garden. Now that I hear many unusual reports from these followers of Jesus, I am only more convinced of the truth of what I witnessed firsthand.

Please be at ease concerning my safety. I remain at this moment in hiding, a very safe distance from Jerusalem, and must continue to do so for some time. I must remain hidden and in the shadows long enough to become a distant memory in the minds of my supervising officers and Pontius Pilate or I am sure I risk arrest and certain death. You must remember that my original commitment to the Roman legions was intended to span some 20 years and Rome does not look favorably on those of its military that fail in their assigned tasks. So, I am as though I am not. I live, yet for a time I am as dead. I must remain hidden. Although I was given a specific word that I would be protected from prosecution, I cannot trust those who promised such help. The promise, which I will explain later, is in itself a betrayal and a lie, given with words that are hollow and vacant. And even more so now, since the current wrestling in my heart and soul have brought me to doubt my decision to be muted and silenced with blood money. As well, I have had forced upon my mind an ever increasing belief that what I saw was true and divinely appointed. I risk exposure in even writing this information to you, but must hope that those who carry this to you can be trusted, and that the delivery of this communication to you will not result in my exposure or your endangerment. I only hope to inform you of my state and clarify for you my involvement in the events that mark the death and it would appear, the resurrection, of this Jesus, whom they call the Messiah.

As I have re-lived those days in my mind continually, and dreamt fiercely about them in fitful bouts of sleep each night, it now seems right to inform you of those same events as I may not see you again. Also I am sure the implications of what I saw will shake the earth and its kingdoms far into the future, and thus I request that you read with an open heart as I convey to you my experience and testimony.

Arriving in Jerusalem, as part of my legion and cohort, was seen by most of my fellow soldiers as a curse. The Jewish people had long proven to be unwilling to cooperate with Rome and thus, Judea and Samaria were in constant turmoil against Caesar. So, being assigned to this out-of-way place in the Roman Empire meant that we were constantly involved in peace keeping and law enforcement duties among a people who largely despised us. They would think nothing of resistance and even violence in order to protect their religious way of life, especially their precious temple, sacrifice rituals, their Law, and their priesthood. We were always on alert for possible unrest and rioting. Although the City of Jerusalem, along with its enormous Temple, and the grand palaces of King Herod commanded a certain respect, and there was occasional beauty to be seen in the Judean desert, most of us legionnaires felt it mostly a primitive place for a primitive people with a primitive religion. It held no real comparison in our minds to the great cities of Rome or Athens. We were here to do our job and not to make the place our home.

I had been in Jerusalem for only two months when the Jewish leaders and general population surrounding Jerusalem became very agitated about a man named Jesus. He had been for some time traveling and preaching in the area and had convinced many, who believed him to be the Jewish Messiah. He had also made many enemies, in particular, many in the Jewish Sanhedrin that felt Him to be a great threat to Judaism. He had been arrested and put on public trial before our honorable Pontius Pilate. In this the Chief Priests had demanded His death due to evidence that He had blasphemed the Temple, the Law and Jehovah Himself. More than once I had been called out with other soldiers, to control large crowds of people who followed this man, and who were worked into political frenzies on numerous occasions, as the Jewish leaders sought to have Him crucified.

Crucified He was, and although I was not assigned to that particular task, I remember the afternoon of His death as being very unusual. The entire afternoon, the final sentencing, His walk to the site of the cross, and His painful suspension above the earth, was enveloped like a smothering blanket by a sudden freakish storm. It seemed to appear from nowhere and dissipate into nothing soon after His death. And at what many soldiers say was the very moment of His last breath, the sky rumbled with thunder and exploded with severe flashes of lightning, and the hill of Golgotha and indeed Jerusalem itself, was shaken with a strong earthquake. It seemed for many of us that the quake was aimed at both the crucifixion sight and the Temple. Reports were that the mammoth curtain protecting the Holy of Holies was literally torn in two at the moment of the earthquake, although I am told that many of the priests from the Jewish temple are reluctant to confirm this. Some say an angel stood over the giant drapery and ripped it down the center with his bare hands at the moment of this man's death. This I do not doubt, having had a glimpse of my own angel just a few days later. Though not a particularly religious man myself, as the afternoon of darkness had progressed, even I at the time thought that we had witnessed the death of no ordinary person. It would not be until several days later that this rather casual observation would be profoundly confirmed.

As the afternoon moved ploddingly into evening, a dark shadow seemed to hang over the whole of the valley, as the city slowly processed the gruesome events of the earlier day. It was here that I became directly involved with the strange and cruel proceedings. I was selected, with several others, to go immediately to the place of the garden tombs to stand guard. We soon learned that we would be standing guard over a closed and sealed tomb. In fact, it was the tomb where the body of this Jesus, the hoped for Messiah, had been placed. We were to guarantee that the tomb remained closed, sealed, and undisturbed. The reason for such instruction we were not told, nor were we told how long we were to stand our position? We only knew that we had direct orders from Pontius Pilate to cooperate fully with the High Priest and elders of Israel.

Finding my position some 30 lengths from the large and heavy stone that stood waiting next to the opening of the tomb, I stood as best as I could at attention, serving as final witness to the burial. The garden itself seemed pleasant enough and posed no unusual strategic threat to a buried body! Stately Olive trees grew in simple order throughout the area and a sober quiet air lay still over the other tombs and other grave markers. Several Jewish men, whose grieving demeanor was not easily hidden, had carried the body of this Jesus, wrapped carefully in strips of burial cloth, down into the dark and cavernous mouth of the tomb. It seemed from my vantage point that they were swallowed by the great tomb. All that could be observed for several moments were faintly flickering lights and muffled voices as the final resting place for the body was made secure in the great hollow.

In the garden, however, huddled to the side of the main entry path, were several women, who made no attempt to hide their sorrow or tears. They mourned and wept openly as the tomb spewed up its visitors, and then with grinding, scrapping, and rasping sounds, the imposing stone closure was slowly rolling over the tombs opening. As the stone and the tomb were sealed, I was paying very close attention, since I was to insure that this tomb remained so until further notice. On either side of the great circular stone, large iron spikes were driven into the adjacent wall, then several tightly wound cords were tied across the stones face and imprinted with several of the seals of Rome. Slowly the parade of officials, priests, mourners, and a few of the curious, dissipated into the shadows of night. Our small team of protectors settled in for our nighttime duty and then waited for our replacements, which would arrive with the morning sunrise of the next day.

The sunrise indeed came and I spent the next day away from the tomb pondering the reasons behind all the official fuss and bother over the burial of this Jewish prophet. Apparently this man had not owned property or maintained any respectable wealth, and nothing was carried into the tomb that I could see would require such great concern about thievery. And if His followers wanted His body for some reason, I did not think it unreasonable to let them have it. What could possibly hurt in such a circumstance? It would be just a matter of a few hours and I would understand the concern and commotion.

I reported for duty in the evening of the second day after the crucifixion and burial, and looked forward to the close of my night watch that would finish at day break of the third day. It seemed to me that with every passing day where nothing took place, the urgency for guarding the tomb would become less and less. Therefore I looked forward to getting one more night behind me and hopefully getting this whole three day festival behind all of us. That of course did not happen. Not only did it never get put behind me, it would prove to be an occurrence of such epic scope, that what I saw and learned of its shocking truth, would be etched into me as if some invisible hand had used a masons blade to carve the surface of my stony heart.

It was sometime in the fourth watch between 3 and 6 am, several hours before daylight that I noticed the air and atmosphere in the garden were changing. It felt as though the heavy dark night was being twisted, churned, lifted, and opened toward the sky above. The garden itself was still quiet in its purpose of honoring its dead, but toward the sealed tomb I felt a kind of energy, an imperceptible surge of strength that only my spirit could actually discern. For several minutes this eerie sensation continued becoming amplified and stronger. It emanated only from the tomb itself! All else in the rest of the garden area remained passive and still. I looked to the other soldiers as if to find some consoling look on their faces that would calm my rising fear. I found none. Instead their faces and eyes were clearly showing the same unease and mounting fright. Terror itself was beginning a slow crawl up our backs and beginning to squeeze our necks and throats. As good soldiers we made every effort to stand stiffly in our places, alternately watching each other, and then looking on to the tomb, hoping to discover the source of this horrible, yet ecstatic sensation.

Suddenly, as if a rising and mounting pressure had reached its appointed moment to burst forth, a blast of light exploded in mid-air in front of the tomb and a blinding, blazing yellow glow slowly took the form of a huge angelic man. Without a single utterance and without noticing any of us, he effortlessly stepped to the side of the giant stone with its seals and markings, and with a single outstretched hand that moved to give only a slight touch of the stone, he rolled it to the opened position. Instantaneously, one of the iron spikes in the wall facing twisted completely in two like soft clay in a potter's hand, and the tightly wound cords that pressed the stone's face split and popped like the overextended straps of an old leather sandal. Then, with the ease of a soft gentle breeze, this glowing angelic man, without taking a single step, drifted upward through the air to the top of the great stone door. With his radiance still pulsating as he moved he sat upon its top edge facing out toward the garden.

At that moment I became frozen, unable to move or speak, the fear that I felt and the glory that filled my vision combined to immobilize any and all of my strength. I would find out later that every other soldier standing with me had the same exact experience. As if this were not enough, at the same time that the angelic being appeared, the ground under us shook violently. It was all I could do to remain standing in the opening minutes of this upheaval. Eventually, I could not maintain the power to stay upright, and almost gladly slumped to the ground, attempting to hide my face from the brilliant light that filled the garden. It seemed the earth itself was assisting the reach of the angelic visitor, so as to shake the tomb open, and expose its contents, its once occupied but now empty space.

What seemed like hours in the making, in reality only took a few brief moments to start and finish. As I knelt in a crumpled pile of raw nerves and emotions, I could faintly hear in the distance the voices of several women. In the fogginess of my own reeling mind I was not sure who was speaking with them or what was the nature of their conversation. In fact, my head screamed inside itself, 'Who could have any kind of conversation after seeing what I just saw!'

I wondered if they had seen what we had just seen. Were they petrified like the rest us?

What was it they were saying? Who was talking with them at this hour of the night?

What was that…this Jesus was no longer buried in this tomb? He was…what?…alive!

An angel had…what?…just opened the empty tomb…was that what I saw?

The darkness quietly regained its dominance over the morning and stillness returned to the garden. A cold slick sweat was attempting to dry on my face and neck.

Had I witnessed…the unheard of…?

Was this Jesus truly alive?

Did He rise from the dead?

Was He leaving behind an empty tomb that I saw opened by an angel from heaven?

As my eyes regained their focus, and my mind settled away from its dread, I instinctively reached to secure my sword and spear. Cautiously bringing my eyes to view the open tomb, I forced my legs to full extension and stood gawking at its reality. My eyes rested on the emptiness of the tomb but my heart refused to rest. It was still pounding in my chest from what I had seen AND from what I had just heard.

I eventually found the courage to look around and attempted to find my fellow guards. None were close by. Two of them, however, who had been the closest to me in the garden, could be seen in the distance. They were beginning to run with all their strength from the scene. I could make out their silhouettes as they moved from olive tree, to fig tree, to grave marker, making their escape across the garden landscape. Without any further thought I was quickly following in their footsteps and disappearing behind them into the early morning mist.

Leaving the garden area I ran as fast as my legs would take me down the first alley way, away from the Tomb. Away from the tomb was the only direction that I wanted to go! Away! Away! Away from this tomb! I was shocked and completely unable to think clearly about what I had just witnessed. I…I…just kept running, around another turn, and into another narrow street. Pursuing nothing, but running like I was being hunted, I ran until my breathless lungs gave out and I could run no further. Gasping for air, and looking for some familiar face or friend, I stumbled along the rough rock walls of the alley, and finally came to a stop in a dark corner of a building. I sat as far into its dark comforting shadow as I could, buried my face in my dirty sleeve, and wept uncontrollably.

My tears were born of fear, terror and confusion. What I had just seen was so real yet could not be so. What had flashed before my eyes was evidence of another world beyond my own and one that I had chosen to ignore all my life. Now, however, I could not deny it was real. I had not been sleeping, not day dreaming, not hallucinating from too much drink. I had stood guard intent to perform my duties and keep all comers away from that tomb. I simply had not in my wildest thoughts expected the tomb would be opened by a visitor from heaven, a mystical, powerful being that did not need or want permission from any human authority to roll back that stone. A visitor from, perhaps the very throne of God, it seemed to me, had broken the deathly calm of that garden grave yard to show the world that this tomb was empty. Empty? I thought to myself. Empty! What did that mean? If anything, it meant that certainly no ordinary person had been put in that dark cavern. A human body may have been carried in, but no one short of a God could break the power of that place and live again!

Quickly my thoughts were forced back to the present. Without warning, I was not alone! Along the dark shadowy street, stumbling along just as I had stumbled, was another unknown figure. He was desperately feeling his way by the same rock wall and now was plunging himself toward my same corner. Before I could move, I found myself face to face with another gasping, panting, terrified soldier. I recognized him. He recognized me. We had both come here fleeing the garden. We both were beside ourselves with confusion and fright. Tongue tied, the moisture of tears and sweat rolling down our faces; we were both unable to completely grasp what had just happened.

Sitting in the stillness for some time, comforted only slightly by each other's company, we said little and looked only down at our trembling hands. What were we to do? Could we simply run and never come back? Would we be able to escape and not suffer punishment? It hardly seemed that escape would be possible. After breathlessly covering our options, we agreed that our only recourse would be to report to the Chief Priests, and explain to them what we had seen. We would tell them exactly what we saw and perhaps there would be sympathy shown to us given the magnitude of our experience. Pulling our heavy bodies to our feet, we immediately made our way through the deserted streets and back alleyways toward the temple. We determined we would find the house of the High Priest and present ourselves to him and the others for their counsel. This, rather than to be hunted criminals, seemed the most sensible thing to be done.

Standing before those Jewish leaders was frightening in itself, not quite as intense as having witnessed the opening of the tomb, but none the less a fearsome event! Each of them in their long robes, their prayer shawls, each with plaited beards and hair, struck alarm and panic in my heart again. We had come in response to our duty and were prepared to tell them all we had seen. But now, with one word of suspicion, we could be sent to the torturers to pay for what could appear to be an extreme derelict of duty.

Well, the entire group sat respectfully as we gave them the details of our ordeal. It seemed to me that the more our story unfolded, the quieter and more resolute they became. Several times stifled gasps of surprise slipped from their lips as some of these leaders reacted to our account. We were asked to sit apart from each other and answer questions designed clearly to expose any discrepancy in our stories. There were none! Our stories were precisely the same and if need be they could send someone to see the tomb for themselves. Without even a request, several leading elders took leave of our group and immediately left for the garden. We assured them over and over again that we had done our duty and were indeed terrorized by our own account. No doubt they could see the fear and dread still freshly present in our eyes and speech. It had been only about two hours since the horrifying events and we were still shaking with its effect. After finishing our account we simply sat on our stools and awaited their counsel.

We watched in silence as the leaders discussed these matters among themselves. I could tell that many who were present were struck with fear and anger at the prospect that there may have indeed been a resurrection. Others seemed interested, even glad! But for the most part the room was filled with a palatable sense of consternation and alarm. For if any of this was even remotely true, and then all of the meticulous plans for the Passover death of this Jesus of Nazareth had failed. I, for one, knew exactly what had happened, and even in facing this formidable group of skeptical Jewish leaders, was beginning to believe in this Messiah, Jesus. The demonstration of power, glory, and sheer majesty there at that garden site gave me too much reality to do otherwise.

Eventually we were called forward by the High Priest, Caiaphas. We simply stood still and waited. What! Were my ears hearing correctly! Was I mistaken! After some time of deliberation and the return of several who had hurried to the empty tomb, we were now being offered a deal. Suddenly, several small bags of money were brought forward and slowly but firmly pressed into our hands. The High Priest and several of the leading elders, we were told, were prepared to speak on our behalf and tell our supervisors and the Governor that the disciples of this Jesus had come in the night and stolen the body away. We were simply asked to comply with their story and insist that this was true, in spite of the implications it had on our reputation and honor. The disciples of this Jesus might be blamed for taking his body, BUT we would bear the embarrassment of being sleepy headed or possibly drunken soldiers. Apparently this was seen as a small price to pay.

My fellow soldier wasted no time in his agreement to the fabrication. The money, the story…it would work for him. I don't blame him. In the state of emotional exhaustion that we were all feeling, this special deal was a welcomed relief. Soon I was swept along in the enthusiasm that began to drift though the room, and found myself holding my money bag, being ushered away from the meeting place, and left in the early morning light just outside the High Priest's residence. In fact, I was left standing alone with only my thoughts and a sense of urgency now building in my spirit.

I could not deny what I had witnessed. I could not live under the shadow of such a falsity and remain true to myself. As a proud Roman citizen and a willing and dedicated member of the greatest fighting force on the face of the earth, I knew I had not failed in my task of guarding the tomb. I had simply been forced to comply with the commands and wishes of a greater authority, one to which all of mankind must answer. I could only see one choice in that moment. I would need to disappear until such a time as my role in this event was either forgotten or forgiven or until the truth of the empty tomb became more accepted among the people of Israel and Rome. It was this thinking that possessed by mind that sad day when I suddenly and abruptly informed you and the others that I could not stay in Jerusalem. At the time I felt it was imperative that I leave for the sake of my own integrity, your safety and to acquire more time to sort out my thoughts and convictions about this Jesus, the Messiah.

In the months that I have been in hiding, I have come to a place of peace in my heart. The empty tomb has forced me to pursue the truth about this Jesus. I must close now, but convey my most heartfelt love for you all; hoping that the news I am now hearing out of Jerusalem, Samaria and even Syria is true. There, I am told, many disciples and followers of this Jesus have seen Him alive, and believe as I do that the tomb is indeed empty.

It is my prayer that you come to this same knowledge as I have, and perhaps together we will be able to pursue this Messiah in the near future.

God speed and Shalom to you all,
Marcus Tertinius Vitalis

CHAPTER FOUR:
THE EXODUS
EXODUS 12-14

Historical background and setting

The year is approximately 1446 B.C. Israel has been in Egypt for 430 years, since about 1875 B.C, when Joseph brought his father Jacob and his entire family back to Egypt to live in the area called Goshen. In the most recent years, the people of Israel have been functioning in the capacity of the Pharaoh's personal labor force. The entire nation has been subscripted into slavery and pressed into the task of building the great structures, palaces, and pyramids of Egypt.

The slavery has been cruel and the work unbearable. In this impossible situation God has heard the prayers and cries of Israel and recruited a hero to challenge Pharaoh and set the people of God free. In this period of time when the Passover is instituted and the People of God are dramatically rescued from Pharaoh and his army, a young Hebrew man tells the story of the exodus from his personal first hand perspective.

The Story

Part One "The Covering"
Part Two "Trapped"
Part Three "The Crossing"

I am a man of Israel, part of the great hoard of people that Jehovah called out of Egypt and delivered by the strength of His own arm through the leadership of his prophet Moses. As a newly married young man given to slavery in the clay pits of Egypt, I was privileged to be included in the first Passover celebration of the Hebrew people, and witness firsthand the journey out of Egypt toward the promised land of Canaan. This is my story.

Part One "The Covering"

The hardships of living in the Sinai desert are really nothing compared to the brutal and impoverished conditions we faced every day in Egypt. And as such it is beyond me as to why so many of my fellow Hebrews find more time to complain than they do to work at insuring our safe passage through this retched wilderness. This wilderness certainly is a crucible of prolonged inconvenience but compared to the cruel bondage of the Pharaoh should be seen as a paradise of sorts. It will give way to the promises of a new land, if we are but faithful and patient! I know it will! The prophet Moses has told us clearly that Jehovah will see us through to the land that flows with milk and honey. It has been only a few short weeks since our great deliverance from Egypt and yet so many of my fellow Hebrews are untrusting and uncooperative in this journey. Moses, no doubt, will find his patience stretched to its furthest length in dealing with these faithless people and their short memories. It is as if they have forgotten everything!

The miracles, the power, the glory, and the fearsome judgments of God on the Egyptians are all still so vivid in my mind. I had only in my thoughts and day dreams seen such dramatic displays of God's power and protection, never in the real world. Even when they were happening all around me, I was forced to pinch myself numerous times to prove to my struggling mind that it was all true! Thinking back and recounting the whole affair still causes my pulse to race and my spirit to soar to the heavens!

I had just been married to my dearest Miriam when news came that a strange prophet from the land of Midian had arrived. We were hearing that He had been sent by God Himself to challenge the Pharaoh; challenge him to let the people of God go free. This seemed most unlikely in my mind, but indeed the news caused a great stir among the elders and the people. Long tiring days and short fitful nights left little time to plan a wedding ceremony in our grand Hebrew tradition, but with the help of family and friends at last we exchanged our vows under the canopy and were united before God. We had only barely been able to find time for our sacred ceremony, since both of us were subscribed to making bricks for the Pharaoh. My precious Miriam spent her long days, exhaustingly scouring the harvested grain fields for straw. This was added to the clay and mud mixture I was preparing daily to make bricks. I longed for those brief moments, when I was able to stop trudging and stomping in the pits, to see her sweet smile as she tossed baskets full of straw at my feet. This straw was stomped and pressed into the muddy slime all day, each and every day, under my bare feet and those of many others. It was those times of exchange that kept our hope of marriage alive and served to comfort each of us even after our union.

Now with the news of this prophet, a fresh source of hope began to rise in our hearts. Was God, at last, going to deliver his people from their humiliation and suffering? As much as Miriam and I were in love and savoring our life together, this possibility of freedom brought a whole new spirit of faith and joy to each of us. At times we were giddy with laughter, thinking of the possibilities.

The months leading up to that sobering night of 'the covering' were filled with incredible, even unbelievable reports, that came in from all across Egypt. Although we, as God's people, were largely protected and secluded in the land of Goshen, we were hearing about spectacular encounters between this Moses and the leaders of Egypt. Plagues of all types were descending upon the land. One week invasive insects and reptiles invaded, another week rivers and streams were turned to blood, then, another week would go by, and fire and lightening would fall from heaven. We were hearing of cycle after cycle of judgments and yet the Pharaoh seemed unmoved. Terrible sores and boils among the Egyptian people developed, for a time wide spread death of livestock and cattle was seen, even destructive hail from fierce sudden storms came down crushing every green growing thing in sight. Finally, before the night of 'the covering' arrived, the entire nation was plunged into total darkness. Even the fires and torches proved to be futile efforts for making light as they were swallowed by this darkness, a thick smothering blackness that could actually be felt. It was a clammy cold gloom. Looking back now, we should have suspected something decisive would follow as the whole nation lay suffering without a hint of light.

Moses, the prophet from Midian, had told us that a final deadly plague was about to come and bring a completion to the judgments that Egypt had experienced. He explained to us, in no uncertain terms, that we were to pack all of our belongings, great or small, and be prepared to leave at a moment's notice. We could not bake bread or leaven our dough, we were to pack and wait with sandaled feet and cloak at the ready. After all the packing was done, we as a nation were to prepare a special meal, centered on a freshly slain and roasted lamb. This meal would then be eaten, while God's final judgment on our Egyptian captors commenced.

We were not sure what this final night would look like, or how it would end, but we certainly felt the urgency and seriousness from the mouth of Moses as he detailed the required aspects of the meal; in particular, the *absolute necessity* of keeping the lamb's blood and marking our dwellings with its fresh red stain. It occurred to me, while hearing these guidelines, that Israelites, all over the country, would be marking their home as a kind of safety zone or rescue station for the night hours. And the marking would be the marking of blood. Indeed the Lamb's blood was to be placed on the upper and two side posts of the door of each house. It did not matter size, or location, or number of inhabitants, it just mattered that the blood of the lamb be on and over each door.

All Israeli family members were instructed to be in their houses and thus under the blood, as soon as the sun would set. It would be then that we would eat our final meal in Egypt, our unleavened bread, the meat of the roasted lamb, just previously killed. Many of our friends invited neighbors to join them and made sure that every family member was present and accounted for before the evening arrived. My new bride and I, along with my widowed mother, and my two brothers, and their families, crowded into our small two roomed house to eat, wait, and wonder!

There was a clear nervous excitement in our home as the night passed. It was impossible to sit still for too long at a time, so we all took turns nervously moving about the packed space. Whether pacing our tiny floor, attempting to peer out our small windows, or standing at the front of the house near the door, we waited. We listened for sounds from the world that lay just outside, beyond our touch. Touch, we dared not, for fear of leaving the safety of our blood covering. The night wore on with increasing tension and apprehension. Although we did not know what this final judgment would actually be, we knew it would be a strike at the first born male of every Egyptian family. It was only at the dawn of the next morning that we would realize how death had touched every family.

As the evening moved into night and the night became deeper and later, fleeting and distant sounds began to drift into our hearing. We were afraid to go outside and unable to see through the night, so we simply listened. At first we were not able to distinguish the sounds, or maybe we did not really want to believe the sound we were hearing. Distant cries, far-off shrieks, far flung pain from a thousand broken hearts, was traveling through the air to meet us. Although the warmth of the fire and the warmth of our love as a family surrounded us, we looked into each other's faces and were intensely aware that everywhere outside of our bloody protection the judgment of God had touched down. Wave after wave of tearful sounds and mourning filtered through our safe haven as the night deepened and turned toward dawn. We were safe and secure under the provision of the blood. A lamb for a family had turned away the curse of death and wrapped us all in the great mercy of God.

As the following day came fully into view and began to brighten with the sunrise, the Egyptian people began to filter slowly out of their homes into the streets and market places. With their grief still fresh on their faces, tears still flowing, and anguish in their voices, they began begging us to leave, to spare them anymore pain and humiliation. They lifted cries in the streets and pleaded with their own leaders to send us away before the entire nation was destroyed.

We waited! We were ready and waiting! As news finally arrived that we were indeed given our freedom, the terrified Egyptians rejoiced and cheered for we had become a curse to them. They so much wanted us to leave that they gave us anything we asked of them; food, clothing, animals; even gold and silver! They were glad to see us go, hoping to find any way possible to see to it that we left them alone and left them as soon as possible.

Part Two "Trapped"

The exhilaration of leaving Egypt behind was more than could be described. The thrill was only tempered a bit by the frantic pace in which we were required to work in order to leave promptly. Since we had been ready to leave the night before, even while the roasted lamb, unleavened bread and bitter herbs were passing through our hungry lips, we were indeed able to move quickly. As we gathered our belongings and filled the streets, we were met by friends, relatives, acquaintances and many complete strangers whose only connection to us was our common Hebrew heritage. The entire Hebrew nation, all at once it seemed, surged forward to rid themselves of their chains. We moved and flowed together like many small streams making one large watercourse, tributaries of humanity pouring into a magnificent and mighty river. Ahead of us were thousands of thousands it seemed and behind us the same. A river of people, animals, small carts, and simple wagons loaded down with everything we owned, progressed as one single people. After over 400 years of suffering we were leaving our bondage behind and traveling forward toward an unknown but welcomed Promised Land.

As we walked, Miriam and I held tightly to each other. She, occasionally squeezing my upper arm gently with her dainty hands and pressing her head and cheek to my shoulder; me stretching my arm out around her brave shoulders to pull her closer to my side, and all the while making sure that my esteemed mother could keep up with everyone. As we made our progress, bursts of laughter and shouts of joy rolled over the crowd like waves of refreshing rain or mist on a hot day. Children danced and darted in all directions as the new freedom overwhelmed their minds and emotions. Everyone helped and watched out for the other as this great massive gathering of people moved further and further away from the stark and stale accommodations of their slavery. The jubilant bellows and daring screams of a free people echoed over and through the people for hours on end as the sheer weight of this new reality settled on all of us. After 400 some years of slavery and abject poverty we were now a free people with miraculous provisions!

Toward the close of the first day of travel an eerie stillness suddenly fell over the people. Conversations quieted to a whisper and the general chatter of thousands of people walking and talking together gave way to a somber hush. There in the distance, toward the front of the masses, no doubt at the point where Moses and Aaron were leading us, began to form a huge column of smoke and cloud. It billowed upward and outward and churned into and out of itself constantly. It seemed that this giant pillar had an energy all its own. At times there could be seen flashes of light and streaks of trailing radiance darting through the thick haze. At first it was reported that a large fire had been started, then it was said that the wind had begun to lift and stir the desert sand into a huge frenzy ahead of us, but as we watched and continued to journey forward, it became obvious that this pillar was traveling with us and not part of the sandy and rocky landscape around us. Soon, emphatic and emotional reports were being passed back to us that the God of Abraham himself was displaying his Shekinah glory to guide us along. I remember looking at Miriam with wide and startled eyes as we were told of this miracle and seeing her return a look of excitement and joy and quiet assurance. "Jehovah is leading his people!" she said. The mere thought brought shivers to my skin and a bright flush to my face.

This became absolutely clear to us when evening began to fall across the desert. Everyone was beginning to find a place to settle for the night and set up make shift accommodations for an over-night stay. Families were gathering, animals were tied securely, and small cooking and warming fires began to appear like glimmering jewels scattered out over the sand as the entire nation of people prepared for night and a quick meal before sleeping. It was at this point that I realized that the night was not deepening as it would on a normal evening. This, as it turned out, would be the first of many abnormal evenings.

The torches and fires that now dotted the scene were losing their edge against the night. Night was indeed falling upon us but we were not being enveloped with the usual loss of light. It was night...BUT it was not... at the same time. I stood up as straight as I could and looked out over the sea of people around me. Miriam had just finished helping my mother with her blankets as she attempted to retire for the night and joined me as I made my search of the night. As our tired and weary bodies leaned together, embraced in the evening haze, we were both caught at the same time by a most amazing view. Pressed against my side with both arms holding tightly around my waist, Miriam gazed with me into the distant glow. Far off in the distance the column of cloud and smoke that had led us out to this stopping point was taking on a different look. Slowly and deliberately it was becoming more brilliant as shimmering hues of yellow and red and orange were starting to billow upward. Up and down the entire length of this gigantic mast of glory illuminating rays of light were spreading out over the people of God. The pillar of smoke by day had become a consuming fire of light by night.

This miraculous change from day to night, from cloud to fire, would become a regular and timely event every day as we traveled ever closer to our promised land. With both of us feeling each other's surging pulses and quickened heart rates, we could do nothing but cradle each other tightly and stare at the billowing flames of God's protection!

On the third or fourth day of movement, we arrived at the place the Egyptians called Pi-hahiroth, situated between Migdol and the sea. We were instructed to camp in front of Baal-zephon, facing it with the sea at our side. This was a curious place to stop, it seemed to me, when not too many miles away we could have taken a much more traveled route to the north, skirted the land of the Philistines, and dropped south again into the land of Promise. This, we would learn soon enough, was not to be. The God of Jacob would have other plans. As the huge river of people slowed to an eventual stop, some became concerned and agitated by our change in direction and the fact that the sea served as a barrier to our progress, perhaps even a trap if for some reason we were attacked! Complaints began to surface among many of my brethren and word was sent to the prophet Moses that many were unhappy with these arrangements. His reply to those who were faint of heart was one of patience and perseverance. We were to watch and wait for God's provision! What developed over the next few hours would be the first great test of trust for the Hebrew pilgrims and sojourners.

It was not long before a greater source of panic would come to us. Several men who had been given the task of scouting the land and watching for obstacles and enemies came running breathlessly into the camp, giving us terrifying news. It appeared that in the distance toward Egypt there was a large disturbance on the horizon. Large plumes of dust and sand were seen rising from the desert as if being driven by some sinister force. It was not long before this force was identified. Pharaoh was on his way! The shock of this news stunned and terrorized us. It was said that he was driving 600 chariots and their men, along with horsemen and soldiers, directly toward us! Panic broke out through the ranks of the people. Women were frantically gathering their children. Men were attempting to gather any item possible that would make for a weapon of defense. Moses and Aaron, we were told, were almost mobbed by a large number of angry men as they shouted something about being taken from Egypt only to dig their graves in the wilderness! People began to scatter, scream and some even tried to hide. Thankfully, many began to cry out to God for mercy as well!

Part Three "The Crossing"

As it was told to me later, those close enough to see Moses, watched in awe as he mounted an outcropping of rock, climbed to a strategic point at the top and looking out over the sea raised his long rod and stretched it as far as it could be stretched toward the rolling waves. Turning in deliberate cadence from the people to the sea and then back to the people he shouted;

"Don't be afraid! Stand firm and see the Lord's salvation He intends to provide for you! These Egyptians will never be seen again after today! Be quiet and watch the Lord fight for you! In the meantime break your camps and be ready to move."

As these last words left his mouth and he stared out over his outstretched rod to the sea, the work of God began. From our vantage point we could see neither Moses nor the shoreline of the sea, but as we watched, the large pillar of glory began to move violently up and over the startled crowds! Churning as it moved and flashing with lightening and fire, it settled out over the desert in the direction of the oncoming armies of Pharaoh. Its placement on the line of the horizon clearly became a defensive barrier between us and the Egyptians. As the armies were blocked from reaching us and even seeing us clearly, the fright and fear on our side of the great fiery barrier began to subside. If what we saw on our side of the barrier was any indication of what Pharaoh and his soldiers saw on their side of the fiery barrier, we had no need to fear. The cloud was now a fiery smoky mass of boiling heat. No one dared approach it for fear of being consumed. There was no doubt in my mind, that in the same way we were strangely comforted by this sight, the armies of Egypt were trembling in their place as they struggled to make sense of this God who fought for His people.

At the time that the Pillar was settling into its protective position against the Egyptians a swirling whirling east wind began to blow out over the sea. At first no one saw this as an unusual thing since strong winds along the sea were regular occurrences but soon it became clear that this wind was divinely placed. In the darkness of night the flaming pillar gave off just enough light that many could make out a bizarre shadowy action taking place out on the water's surface. Two separate lines of bubbling waves and foam were forming side by side, stretching out across the water from the shore, into the distant blackness of the sea. As each hour passed these lines of roiling, splashing waves moved further apart and the wind seemed to pile water up and backwards behind each line of waves. It was creating what looked like two parallel and ever increasing heights of water. Gazing into the night, the mist of the driving sea seemed to reveal two huge walls of water forming in the sea that looked as if they were extending as far as the eye could see into the depths. Few people were able to sleep with the east wind howling over the water, the stirred up waves making a constant dull roar of sound, and the great pillar of fire crackling its resistance against our Egyptian foes. It would prove to be that the God of Abraham, Isaac, and

Jacob was in the process of making a way of escape for a bewildered, but grateful people.

As the first hint of daylight attempted to push through the early morning grayness, word was already being sent through the entire camp of partially sleeping but mostly vigilant Hebrews. At the command of Moses we were to resume our journey on to the Promised Land. Which direction was he taking us? The pillar of fire still covered our rear flank and the chariots and soldiers were still hidden, although at times some thought they could see movement through the flames. It was clear that retreat was out of the question. If we were to go now we would have no choice but to find a way across the water of this great sea. Unless, of course, by some miracle we could go through it! Well…indeed we would!

As the air cleared and the sun assisted us with more light we began to make out an unbelievable sight! There in front of us, at the edge of the shoreline was a great cavernous opening that extended out onto the sea bed. Looking out into this watery gateway we could see exposed rock and sand reaching all the way across to the far side of the sea. At the command of our leaders and without hesitation, people in every direction began to run down into the sea bed. In some cases cumbersome items and heavy gear were abandoned for the sake of better travel, but for the most part we simply gathered our belongings and walked out onto the sand. What a strange and odd sensation to be walking on the dry bottom of a once very wet body of water.

This time there was little conversation or idle chatting. Previous shouts of joy and victory had given way to sighs, whispers and muted expressions of shock, dismay, and gasping. People were in awe of what they were seeing. Standing on each side of our broad nautical pathway was nothing but water, water that stood high like vast cliffs of shimmering quivering glass. Immediately we felt the cold moist air surround us as we plunged deeper into the bowels of the empty sea. Many, especially children, moved to the edge of the water as they stepped forward and plunged their hands into the wall, only to quickly jerk backward in reaction to the wet and cold water. The east wind could be seen blowing hard over the tops of the two high cliffs of water. Spray and mist would trickle softly down upon us from time to time as we walked between these tall water sentinels. The walls of deep blue and green water, with its hints of swirling current, seem to be guiding forward and pointing the way to the other side. As we walked and gazed at the walls of water, Miriam would shriek or squeal now and then at seeing what she thought sure was a fish or sea creature staring back at us as we moved past. The entire nation of Israel moved with a corporate awe and sense of thrill along the sandy ocean bottom and did so without so much as a single sandal or clothing hem getting wet.

There was really no time to spend exploring this vast underwater world. We were intent on getting across to the other side and hoping that somehow the armies of Egypt would decide against following us through our salty channel to freedom. This hope was short lived as soon it became clear that the chariots, horsemen and foot soldiers were being commanded to pursue us. Looking back in the direction of the once entrenched column of fire and cloud we could see that our pillared guard had forsaken our rear defense. As quickly as we could we directed people in every direction up the beach to more secure footing, and looking back out across the open expanse of sand could see the last of our people were making their way up and out of the channel in the sea. The pillar of cloud and fire no longer prevented our enemies from marching after us. It was lifting, as the last of our people emerged from the bottom of the sea bed, and this time, it was moving quickly and silently over the top of us to the dry land above our exit point.

Straining to look out across the open cavern of the sea, we could see the chariots circling on the other side, and the horsemen attempting to calm their horses, before they dashed into the opening that lay before them. The foot soldiers assembled and gathered courage to join the rush into the dry bottom of the great sea. As if the last few days of turbulent emotions were not enough, now we faced a sudden crush of fear again with the immediacy of Egypt's finest military poised to swoop down on us. It was obvious that they planned to borrow our way of escape and turn it into another trap and it seemed all we could do was watch in exhaustion.

As the armies began making their way into the heart of the sea there was a sudden stirring in the Pillar of Cloud. As if reacting to the urgent turn of events or perhaps imparting knowledge and wisdom to Moses, the Shekinah intensified in its brilliance and for several moments it appeared that God Himself was making a decisive assessment of the situation. On the other side of the water the soldiers were suddenly having difficulty moving into the open channel. Chariots were losing wheels; horses were stumbling or refusing to continue; soldiers were unable to move quickly as the water table in the ocean floor began to rise and soften the sand beneath their feet. It appeared that confusion was spreading over the Egyptian hoard. Now with a slow but deliberate motion, our leader, Moses, turned toward the sea and the oncoming armies of Egypt. It was clear that he knew exactly what he was to do. Jehovah had spoken to our leader and he was about to take action!

With all eyes on the prophet we collectively held our breath watching his silent command. He steadied himself against the still blowing wind without fanfare or drama; he simply raised his rod of God toward the oncoming soldiers, horses and chariots. As he did, the high glimmering walls of water began to shake and drop, as if melting under the pressure of the outstretched rod. The dry sea bed quickly filled with water, trapping the advancing army in its tracks. As the force of the east wind relaxed its grip on the cliffs of water they began to tumble from the top and crash back down into the open spaces of the cavern below. In doing so deep, permanent, and watery graves engulfed those who were trapped below. As the full weight of the sea came rushing back into its place the armies of Egypt were drowned, buried and left spinning in the waves, only later to be washed ashore as refuge from a great defeat.

The people of God were left speechless. We were stunned but relieved. None of us could find words to express our reaction at first. Many simply cried quietly as the waters of the great sea sloshed and splashed and finally settled into calm. Families gathered and took stock. People were searching for friends and comforting those who were overwhelmed with emotion. Slowly but surely the reality of our freedom settled upon us. Quickly shouts of joy and praise began echoing from the shoreline out over the watery divide. Soon enough we would be dancing and singing for joy, but at this moment all we could do was slowly breathe in the air of our new found freedom and relish the mercy and loving kindness of the God of Israel.

Just a few days earlier we had been a people without a home, trapped in Egypt without a leader and some even thought we had been permanently abandoned by God. But through the protection of a blood covering, God had faithfully responded to the cries of His people. He had sent a deliverer, brought low the proud Egyptians, destroyed their armies and brought an entire nation through the flood of the sea. All of this to bring us out of our land of bondage and start us on our way toward the Promised Land. We, who were not a people, were set apart as a people, by the strength of God's power! We who were not a people were now God's people!

DOUGLAS S. MALOTT

CHAPTER FIVE:
FELLING A GIANT
1 SAMUEL 16/17

Historical background and setting

The year was approximately 1050-1000 B.C. the Israelites have just requested a king to rule over them and the Prophet Samuel has anointed Saul as King over the nation. After several minor battles and skirmishes with the Philistines, Israel finds themselves in a military standoff. The Israeli army is being challenged by a Philistine giant named Goliath and no one has the confidence to challenge him in hand to hand combat. It is at this stage in the ongoing humiliating scene that an unlikely hero steps forward. As the scenario now changes to Israel's advantage a member of their army tells the story.

The Story

The business of war is a dismal venture. Even if one is victorious, the victory can come at a very high price. The price of losing fellow soldiers to the sword, the possibility of being personally wounded or scarred in a way that would mark you for the rest of your life…was not something we as foot soldiers were accustomed to thinking about or discussing among ourselves. For the most part, we concentrated on being ready to fight and staying focused on our enemy; although the likelihood of such loss haunted us all.

It had been our tradition for some time to practice as much intimidation as possible before a single blow was thrown, a single arrow was released, or a single war cry was uttered. In order to accomplish this, our entire army would assemble in full battle array within full view of the opposing side. Armor, weapons, banners, soldiers—all placed in multiple long arching columns—spread decisively in front of the enemy. Those on the front line were the biggest, the fiercest, the most skilled and the most experienced. Their mere presence signaled the capability and confidence of the fighting force on display.

Being a part of the Israeli army was a source of great pride for all of us; in particular we lived for the honor of defending our King and our people. At this point in time, I had served several years for King Saul and had on many occasions experienced the thrill and horror of the sudden charge on an enemy position as we wrenched ourselves from the comfort of that powerful 'array display'.

Not being considered large enough for front line service, I had nonetheless run to the battle behind the more grizzled and callused soldiers of that elite forward position, watching with amazement and awe as they cut and pushed and drove their way into the oncoming enemies. Waving sword and thrusting spear, I did my best to push the opposition back and make way for more of my fellow soldiers to come in behind and continue the drive forward.

Today was expected to be no different. The

Philistines had gathered on a small rise across the Valley of Elah from us in the early morning haze. We heard them before we saw them, as the sound of leather and steel rolled over the rocks and low growing shrubs to our ears. We knew instantly that they were preparing to fan out their forces in a similar show of military might.

At the first sound, we had been instructed to gather in our assigned formations and be ready for the viewing when the early mist cleared, as each army sized up the other. Having done exactly that, we waited and watched, secretly hoping that what we were about to see would be obviously inferior to how they perceived us!

As the sun rose higher in the sky to our left, the Philistine Armies could be seen extending across the other side of the valley, reinforcing their frontline warriors with all that was needed to make the initial plunge toward us. Having witnessed it all before in previous battles, it was exactly as we'd expected. **What happened next was not!** In fact, it would set us back on our emotional heels and strain our confidence even before we started. Moving through the ranks of men and pressing toward the front of the formation was a most unusual and shocking creature. Amidst the cheers and shouts of all, a giant of a man was making his way forward and down to the center of the valley floor.

His large, lumbering feet pushed dust up into the air as if the weight of ten men were slapping the ground! Broad shoulders, huge arms and massive hands served only to reinforce his fierceness. On his enormous head was a bronze helmet, his stout trunk-like legs were wrapped with bronze shin guards and the solid bronze sword he'd slung up and over one shoulder glinted in the morning sun as he swaggered. He carried a spear that resembled a weaver's beam with what appeared to be a heavy iron point at its tip. At nearly 10 feet from head to toe, this gigantic human being made his armor bearer, who labored with the monster's shield in front of him, seem small and insignificant by comparison.

We were now seeing what we had previously believed to be mere rumors and strange tales. The champion of the

Philistines, Goliath of Gath, had presented himself and within moments a slow worrisome gasp began to spread through our ranks like a fire set to dry stubble. Soon the audible dread dwindled to silence as we stared out over the valley at this fearsome and eerie sight. At any moment, we expected the colossal soldier to command a charge and lead his followers up into our ranks. But he did not! Instead, he planted his massive frame and his voice began to thunder across the field:

"Why do you come out to line up in battle formation?" "Am I not a Philistine and are you not servants of Saul?" "Choose one of your men and have him come down against me. If he wins and kills me, we will be your servants. But if I win and kill him, then you will be our servants and serve us!"

Then with a final cry the Philistine shouted, "I defy the ranks of Israel today. Send me a man so we can fight each other!" When we heard his threats and assessed our chances, we shrank back in cowardly fear. And though rendered physically incapable of moving, our hearts retreated within us as far away from this Philistine as one could mentally go. Even our king, Saul himself, hid in his tent as he contemplated our next move. Terrified and humbled, what little courage we had mustered in the early morning mist now drained away like so much water from a cracked jug.

As if it wasn't bad enough to be humiliated on the first day of the proposed battle, the Philistine giant came to the same spot on the valley floor to bellow the same tormenting challenge for 40 days! Each morning and evening his belligerent mocking echoed across the valley over our heads.

The sun's rising would greet his first approach, while the moon's rising would greet his last. His piercing and angry words cut each of us to the heart, yet no one could find the courage to step forward. Oddly enough, no one even considered the need for divine help.

Goliath was not only mocking the armies of Israel, he was mocking the God of Israel. And none of us, from the King down to the lowest servant, found the faith or courage to defend the name of Jehovah. Day after day not a single one of our Hebrew thousands who marched into position with well-timed battle cries made any movement to meet this foe fearing the swift and certain death that would undoubtedly follow. Instead, the daily badgering continued unabated.

Yet, throughout those agonizing 40 days, developments were taking place that none of us could possibly have seen coming. While we sat stunned and petrified, David, a young shepherd boy from the Bethlehem area had traveled to the battle front with supplies for his three oldest brothers and the King, as well. The young shepherd's brothers had willingly joined the fight some time ago to support King Saul and although each was a strong and able warrior in his own right, not one of them elected to step forward, either. I had watched several times as David cautiously made his way through the waiting soldiers.

Moving from one group to another and carefully side-stepping weapons and supplies, he brought special greetings and fresh food from home to his brothers at the request of their father, Jesse. During this delivery process, I couldn't help but notice his obvious irritation at the words of the Philistine. His young frame stiffened with anger and annoyance; he would often stare defiantly at this uncircumcised embarrassment while bristling at the sardonic tone of his words.

On one occasion, David could hold his peace no longer. Voicing his frustration to those nearest him, his words cut through the gloom like a sword:

"This pride and arrogance is a disgrace to Israel!"
"Why isn't something being done?" he questioned.

At this outburst of loyalty and criticism, his oldest brother, Eliab, stepped squarely in front of him, pointed his finger in David's face, and rebuked him. Eliab accused his younger brother of childish disrespect and curiosity over the serious matter of war.

He then insisted that David take both his feeble

supplies and concerns and head for home to the job he was more qualified to handle...tending their father's sheep.

Clearly embarrassed at his very public rebuke, David slowly left his brothers and drifted back into the ranks of the retiring soldiers. As he did so, he made one last inquiry concerning the reward the king had offered for defeating Goliath.

It had been announced earlier that King Saul promised riches, exemption from paying taxes AND the hand of his daughter in marriage to the one who could kill this giant; but no one had yet stepped forward to attempt it. The 40 days of humiliation had simply continued! This time as David left the battle field, he did so with what could only be described, in my mind, as a mounting righteous indignation. As it so happened, several soldiers who had overheard young David's complaints and questions about the reward sent word to King Saul.

They reported that a young man named David, from Bethlehem, seemed as though he might be ready to fight this Philistine! Immediately David was summoned before the King. Being in close proximity of the King's royal tent, I moved as close as I could to watch this bizarre scene unfold. A shepherd boy was about to offer the King his service in fighting this giant. Would the King accept? Did he really believe that this young and inexperienced lad could accomplish the impossible?

King Saul sat well behind the front line of action. His throne had been carried to the battle scene and placed in the royal tent just ahead of his arrival. There the King sat, brooding, under several layers of luxurious purple and blue textiles that were stretched and hung overhead to give him adequate shade and protection. Surrounded by his captains and leaders, he alternately complained to and conferred with them as to the urgent matter that faced his army. His face, chiseled with worry, illustrated the strain and pressure of the situation at hand. And then, David was brought before the king. As he entered the royal tent, a hush fell over the entire collection of officers, servants, and advisors alike. The shepherd's very presence stood in stark contrast to the mounting tension in the air.

Some were quieted by the possibility of a volunteer actually stepping forward to take on the giant. Most were stilled by the shock of a young shepherd boy being presented to the King for the daunting assignment, rather than the strapping soldier that they likely expected. As the mood turned more pensive, the King motioned for David to step forward, but before he could lower his hand to his lap, the shepherd boy addressed the King boldly:

"Don't let anyone be discouraged by him, sire; your servant will go and fight this Philistine!"

The King looked young David over from the top of his ruddy head to the bottom of his strong and seasoned legs and feet. In fact, all eyes were on the young lad as they wondered at his confident demeanor. It was clear to me that the King was unsure as to what this young shepherd could do in a confrontation with a warrior twice his size. With furrowed brow and narrowed eyes, the King responded: "You can't go fight this Philistine. You're just a youth, and the giant has been a warrior since he was young".

But his stern reply did not seem to faze David in the slightest. He simply continued as he had begun, explaining with unbridled enthusiasm how on more than one occasion he had defended his father's sheep from wild animals. The shepherd chronicled his encounters with both a lion and a bear as they attempted to take lambs from the flock, he explained in great detail how he grabbed the predators by their furry coats, struck them, and killed them.

Then, in the same breath he confidently assured the King that the fate of this uncircumcised Philistine would be no different! What he said next, however, proved to be the turning point of the entire conversation. It was David's prediction of victory that made this shepherd boy different from the rest...and perhaps qualified:

"The LORD who rescued me from the paw of the lion and the paw of the bear will rescue me from the hand of this Philistine." King Saul looked around at his advisors. No one spoke. At last, after several moments of thought, he turned to David, smiled slowly and commended him to the battle: "Go, and may the Lord be with you," the King replied.

As David turned to leave, several of King Saul's personal servants blocked his exit, running to him with a full dress of armor —armor that Saul himself had worn. A bronze helmet was quickly put on David's head. A coat of armor and the great sword with its belt and sheaf were strapped around his waist. David looked like a soldier; and for those in the royal tent he now appeared much better prepared to defend Israel than he had only moments before. But as the young shepherd attempted to take several steps, he faltered. For a few brief moments David seemed awkward and unsettled as he struggled to move freely under the weight of the armor. The sword was too heavy and quite obviously unmanageable. Though he struggled to make the armor work to his advantage, after several minutes of futile effort he slowly dropped the sword and slipped its belt and sheaf to the ground.

Next, he loosed the coat of armor and let it fall to the as well. Finally, he lifted the bronze helmet from his head and placed it on the other pieces of armor beneath him. He would have to face the giant without the King's battle gear. David could not afford to fight in unfamiliar and untested armor; he would fight with what he knew best.

Moving quickly to the edge of the tent at its front opening and stepping outside, David reached for his shepherds' staff. Then, looking around the area he saw a large steep-sided empty watercourse, dry and parched from the summer heat snaking down the side of the hill behind the area where the Hebrew armies stood watching.

In its crevices were nestled many well-washed stones made smooth by years of turbulent, rushing water. David examined them and then quickly gathered five of the smoothest stones he could find and placed them in his shepherd's pouch. Finally, he gathered up his leather sling, tugged and snapped the two long handle pieces as if to give them one final test, and turned in the direction of the battle front.

At this, I was taken aback. For 40 days no one had

made a single effort to step forward against this enemy and now a shepherd boy with a sling, several smooth stones, and a shepherd's staff was approaching this giant of a man. How could this not turn out to be a tragic mistake, not to mention an embarrassment to our King and the guarantee of slavery for an entire nation! As we watched in astonishment, we could see the look of determination on the young David's face. There was not a hint of fear or hesitation in his movement. At first, he walked slowly out from among the mass of soldiers and attempted to ignore their looks of concern and amazement. But soon, as he made his way clear of their gaze, he began to run toward the valley floor.

At this sign of movement on our side of the valley, the great champion of Gath began to move forward to position himself for the kill. Like a bull before the charge, his footsteps pounded the ground as he snorted and moved in the direction of the small figure now running toward him from Israel's ranks.

As the two approached each other the great Goliath stopped, raised his massive spear and groaned loudly. It appeared to us that he was agitated by this handsome, healthy and youthful shepherd turned warrior.

"Am I a dog that you come against me with sticks?" he snarled.

The derisive question was immediately followed by a steady stream of vile and filthy words as he cursed David in the name of the Philistine Gods, Beelzebub, 'Lord of Flies' and Dagon, "Lord of the Land'. White-hot with fury at the Hebrews' insinuation that a mere boy could defeat him he became enraged to the point of delirium!

"Come here," the Philistine demanded with bared teeth and strained voice "and I will give your flesh to the birds of the air and the wild beasts!"

David did not hesitate. With a surge of faith and confidence he roared back, "You come against me with a dagger, a spear and a sword, but I come against you in the name of the Lord of Hosts, the God of Israel's armies. Today you have defied Him! Today, the LORD will hand you over to me. Today, I'll strike you down, cut your head off, and give the corpses of the Philistine camp to the birds of the sky and the creatures of the earth. Then the entire world will know that Israel has a God, and this whole assembly will know that it is not by sword or by spear that the LORD saves, for the battle is the LORD's. He will hand you over to us."

With that declaration, David quickly ran to the battle line to meet his foe with his sling and a pouch full of smooth stones while Goliath strode toward him with sword and spear raised above his head. The next few minutes seemed interminable, as if time were at a standstill. The entire armies of both nations drew one, long corporate breath and waited the outcome. Victory for the one and servitude for the other were at stake!

As the Philistine champion lumbered slowly but steadily forward with his fiery eyes focused on his unlikely opponent, David stopped. With the confidence of a shepherd protecting his sheep, he sized up his foe with a determined glance. Reaching into his pouch, he took a smooth stone in his capable hand and placed it snuggly in the sling's carrier.

Seconds later, with seamless and furious motion, he began swinging the secured stone in ever-widening, ever stronger circles over his head. With precise timing, David loosed his hold on one end of his sling and flung the stone with deadly accuracy in the direction of the approaching champion.

Rocketing through the air with dizzying speed as if guided by an invisible hand, the stone turned and twisted as it sped to its target and found its mark. Piercing the forehead of the startled giant, it sank deeply into the meat of his skull.

From our vantage point, it appeared that some unseen force had jabbed a mortal blow upon the Philistine Giant, for indeed he stopped dead in his tracks, stunned and motionless. A brief moment later, like a felled tree of Lebanon, he slowly crumpled to his knees and then pitched forward on his face as the dust of the ground flew up around his listless body. The champion of Gath had fallen and was dying.

As the dust settled on the now lifeless form, the inhabitants of the valley on both sides of the narrow passage way gasped with shock. Instantly, the Philistine army lost all courage and strength while the army of Israel pulsed with a new found faith and a call to arms. David, in the mean time, ran to the fallen giant, grabbed the Philistine's own sword and pulled it from its sheaf. Plunging it deeply into his neck, he severed his head and held it high for all to see!

Seeing that their hero was dead, the entire hoard of Philistines began to run. The men of Israel and Judah, on the other hand, rallied. They shouted their battle cry and plundered the enemy's camp. With a great slaughter, they chased the Philistines to the entrance of the Valley of Elah and to the very gates of Ekron. Philistine bodies were strewn all along the Shaaraim road to Ekron and Gath, as well.

It was a great and defining victory for Israel and for the young shepherd boy from Bethlehem. In the years to come this unlikely hero whose faith in God turned the tide of battle, would reign in Judah and Israel. And with a heart after God's own heart, David would prove to be the greatest king in all of Israel's history.

DOUGLAS S. MALOTT

CHAPTER SIX:
THE WIDOW OF NAIN
LUKE 7:11-17

Historical background and setting

The village of Nain was located in the southern Galilee area of first century Palestine. Located along an open valley across from Nazareth it was secluded and tranquil in its connection to the rolling hill country surrounding the Lake of Galilee. Galilee and the city of Tiberius was a day's walk to the north and east of Nain. Jesus and his disciples had traversed this area in their travels to and from Jerusalem and while moving to and from the coastal areas, but apparently made only one stop at this small town.

The Story

I am a Hebrew widow. I have been one for some time, having lost my husband to sickness many years ago. Although a widow, I was fortunate to not be alone; being the proud mother of a wonderful son, a true gift from God.

This was not the case for others of course; some widows in Israel were both without husband and without sons. I considered myself a blessed woman to have a son who made every effort to care for me and work faithfully in our village.

Nain was not a large village but it had been well suited for me and our family for many years. Situated across the valley from Nazareth, it was located off the beaten path and well away from any major roads that connected us with larger cities.

Ours was a peaceful existence being many miles north of Jerusalem and thus far away from the political and religious turmoil that often found its way into our hallowed capital city.
We were much closer to the great Sea of Galilee, its fishing business and the quiet grazing lands of the surrounding hills.

It was in this context that I had my first personal encounter with the man Jesus. This encounter I am about to describe was a much, much needed and often hoped for encounter, since I had oft been told of the prophet that had come from Nazareth. I had heard of his teaching and of the power that worked through him and since he grew up across our valley we considered him one of our own. I just did not think for a moment that I would meet him in my village and in the very center of some of the darkest days of my life. You see, I had never expected that sickness would strike my family again. During those days when I had watched my beloved husband succumb to an unexpected illness, my heart had been convinced that this curse would be left behind me and I would live without its sinister visit again. This was not to be so!

It was in the weeks following the Pentecost Festival that my son became ill. At first he continued to work, but with his strength failing slightly each week. Finally, after many weeks of labored effort, he could work no longer and soon was confined to the straw mat that eventually became his death bed. In those final days of his dying the entire village surrounded us with their care and concern, providing for our every need and preparing for the inevitable moment when we would carry my son to his grave.

The day of his burial the whole village, it seemed, came to join our procession. As was our custom, the body of the deceased was carefully washed and cleaned, wrapped in linen and then laid on a small bed to be carried to the site of the burial. Several of the leading men in the village were carrying the body of my son, in full view of all, right down the main roadway of the village to the front gate and out to the family plot. Many of our ancestors' remains had been buried in the same manner. As we wove our way through the tiny maze of paths and streets, more and more people came from their homes to join us.

Before long, a huge crowd of friends, acquaintances, village people and the curious swelled up around us. I was touched and humbled by the outpouring of support and care, but most of my attention was on the lonely lifeless form that lay under the burial cloth. My son was dead and soon was to be buried. My heart ached. My eyes poured out tears and anguish and hopelessness. Now I was really alone. Although the gracious people of Nain would seek to help, I was still now very alone. The sight of my unmoving son and the crushing weight of my own aloneness made the scene around me gray and without form. It seemed I was moving in slow motion and hearing nothing but my own cries and groans as we slowly crept toward my son's final resting place. Others were wailing and grieving with me as the throng moved forward but I did not hear their effort being overwhelmed by the sound of my own sobbing.

At some point after we had passed through the city gates out onto the connecting road to Tiberius, I became aware that the mob of mourners had slowed to a standstill. In my foggy state of sorrow, I could not imagine why this was happening and if perhaps, something was wrong with our processional. It was then that a clear piercing voice split through the haze of my broken heart. A voice I had not heard before, but a voice that somehow I seemed to recognize, or at least one that called deeply to my heart and brought it to full attention.

'Please do not weep!' I heard him say. As the words settled into my mind I found the atmosphere become clear and pristine. His words settled my thoughts and gave me a second chance to lift myself above the darkness of the moment. I could now see a man approaching those who carried my son's body.

This seemed odd, but in my state of mind I could do little but watch and silently question this unusual development. Would there be an interruption, a conflict, a disruption in our plans? He moved up next to their circle, intercepting them as they balanced their breathless load. Then, stepping between two of them, He took hold of the edge of the bed. Suddenly I knew that the prophet from Nazareth was here. I could not understand why, I simply knew it was him. His steady look, his humble mannerisms, his visible concern all said to my heart that is was him. Taken back by the teacher's actions, the pallbearers quickly came to a full stop. Since a significant number of people had been walking with the teacher as they were traveling past our village, the combined mass of people set the stage for grand viewing of the glory of God.

I, of course, had no inkling of what would transpire next; I simply was caught up in the swirl of change and compelled to cooperate with the authority of this bold man of God. He had stepped into my life with an outpouring of compassion and concern and now was poised to take action in a way that would startle all of us, exhilarate several and confuse others. What his action meant for me, needless to say, cannot be adequately put into words. The great loss of my life and gaping tear in my heart, as a result of it, was about to be restored. The crowd now became a mixture of squabbling voices, unconvinced mourners, zealous protectors and excited revelers.

This cacophony of sound and emotion came to a sudden halt when the teacher's voice cut through it all and spoke to the corpse of my beloved son on his burial bed, 'Young man, I tell you, get up!' he said, projecting his voice purposely over the full length of the lifeless form.

I was not sure what was going though the mind of others at that very moment, but I was certain that I had not heard him correctly. Had he said…'get up' like I thought he had said? Yes, those where his exact words!

This prophet teacher stood looking over my son's body. The crowd pressed forward to hear and see everything that was happening and I stepped between two of the men holding the bed. I was looking with a side glance at what effect these words might have on the proceedings and on the lovely form under the linen covering.

I had no more turned my head to watch when I saw vividly the face under the cloth press upward into the underside of the blanket material and begin to lift from the bed surface in an attempt to sit up. At the same time, once dead and lifeless arms became active and tugged backward to bring the elbows under the growing weight of my son's strong chest, neck and head! The linen cloth could now not hold down the life that was surging beneath it. It gave way and slid downward folding over itself, as a fully alive and fully upright animated man sat up straight on the bed, now creating more strain for the bed carriers who held tightly to his much heavier body. It was at this point that I heard the most beautiful of sounds. My son was calling my name and asking for me to come to his side. Instantly I stepped near the edge of the bed and pulled his neck toward me as he stood full length on his two reenergized legs and wrapped his quivering arms and hands around me. We embraced long and hard.

After literally attempting to absorb this moment of my son's embrace, over the edge of his garment, I could see the teacher with his hand open and extended as if to present me with a prized gift. My son was raised from the dead and given back to me from the dark abyss of hell! The sentence of death on my son and of a lonely life of solitude for me had been cancelled by the touch and the words of this man of God.

I was exhilarated, ecstatic and almost delirious with joy and hope. The crowd around me was hushed momentarily with reverence, fear and awe. Then spontaneously, many began pressing in upon us reaching to touch the miracle man and embrace us both while praising and glorify the God of Israel.

One man shouted, to the glee of the mass of people that surrounded us, 'God has visited us!' Another proclaimed to the agreeing flock of supporters, 'Indeed, a prophet has risen among us!' Our embracing and dancing with joy continued with great enthusiasm for some time and carried us naturally back toward our humble village.

It was only after we had reached familiar surroundings near our home that we realized the teacher and his disciples were not among us. He had seemed to have come out of nowhere to bring this miracle to us and now he was gone; gone, we supposed, to another place, where the glory of God was needed. However, his vanishing presence and quick departure did not dull our memory of that day. Throughout all of Judea this report of his work here at Nain was spread like wild fire: A burial march had become a welcome home party because the Nazarene preacher had come!

CHAPTER SEVEN:
PAUL IS SHIPWRECK ON MALTA
ACTS 27

<u>Historical background and setting</u>

The year was approximately 62 A.D. and Paul the Apostle had been placed under arrest by the Roman authorities in Jerusalem, due to the fact that he had been beaten and accused of violating several of the Hebrews sacred laws in regard to the Temple. While under arrest a plot to murder him was uncovered and a decision was made to move him by armed guard to Caesarea Maritima on the Mediterranean Sea. After formal complaints and several hearings were aired before the Roman magistrates, Paul appealed his case to Caesar and was ordered to Rome under the supervision of a certain Centurion named Julius. The story of this voyage to Rome is recorded in the 27th chapter of the Book of Acts of the New Testament.

The Story

My name is Julius. I am a Roman Centurion charged with transporting several prisoners to Rome, one of whom happened to be the Apostle Paul. This is my story. One aspect of military service that is most unenjoyable is the dangerous business of transporting prisoners. Although it can be seen as an honor to be entrusted with prodding criminals to their final destination for trial, imprisonment or perhaps execution; I was not enamored with the duty. I, Julius, had serviced the Caesar for many years; in fact, I served several different Caesar's, while fulfilling my sacred tribute to the great Roman Empire. However, I would have much rather spent my time in the field where the action of war, or at least training for it, was my primary focus. It was for such action that I had been trained. But now with most of the Empire's boundaries secure, the Roman legions were given the task of keeping the peace and enforcing law and order, particularly in areas like Judea where many of the Jews were intent on overthrowing Rome's control and supervision. It was in this capacity that I had been assigned to the city of Caesarea Maritima, on the beautiful shores of the Great Sea. The Emperor himself had dispatched me to the area from where I had been serving him directly in the royal palace. As a centurion, I had 100 of Rome's finest soldiers serving under me and together we provided a formidable force when gathering up malcontents and other prisoners.

It was in conducting these duties that I first encountered the man Paul of Tarsus. While gathering and processing prisoners for our eventual sailing trip to Rome, I had been contacted by the officials of Governor Festus and given one more common criminal for transport by ship to the courts of Rome. Little did I know at the time, this man Paul was anything but a common criminal! In fact, I would come to believe through a series of extraordinary events, that he was truly a man of God, dedicated to his faith and no doubt wrongly accused and wrongly sentenced to jail. Coming to this conclusion would be no easy task. But I would eventually be persuaded by the terrifying process of a very long voyage, enduring a devastating storm at sea and barely escaping a life threatening shipwreck. In the end, after seeing what I saw, there was no doubt in my mind about who he was or what God he served. I only wished in the end that I had not needed to deliver him to Rome, especially since his God had delivered me from the throws of death.

After several weeks of preparation and searching, I was able to secure a transport ship from the port of Adramyttium, that was scheduled to make several stops along the east and north shores of the Great Sea as it made its way closer to Rome. The vessel from Adramyttium was a medium sized ship and designed to carry cargo on short distance voyages along the coast, thus escaping the dangers of the open sea. As was usual for these kinds of voyages we would travel as far as we could on the available ship, then make arrangements later for another ship to carry us further up the coast line toward our final destination.

We left Caesarea and made a short trip to the City of Sidon, just up the coast a half days voyage. Here we waited while cargo was exchanged and additional provisions were secured. It was here that I first encountered several of Paul's friends. These so called 'Christians' were very gracious to their friend and his traveling companions, requesting permission to house this Paul until the time arrived to set sail. Not seeing any real threat from these kindly people, I sent Paul and his small partly, along with two soldiers, to stay in the city until we were ready.

In two short days we put out to sea. Captain, crew, Paul with his companions, the other prisoners, as well as my restless soldiers readied for a longer trip. Sailing west directly out of port we encountered contrary winds, making our hope to skirt under the island of Cyprus only a dream. Immediately we were forced to track with the winds and sail along the northern shore of the big island. Perhaps if I had been paying attention to the signs, I would have seen in this first change of plans a more foreboding warning. But since I did not, we simply plunged ahead toward a strange and frightening destiny. After sailing, with much resistance, through the open sea off the coast of Cilicia and Pamphylia, we reached the port of Myra in Lycia.

It was here that I was forced to contract another ship, since our previous one was not on schedule to meet our transport needs to Rome. A quick survey of the available ships brought me to an Alexandrian ship with a huge cargo of wheat and miscellaneous supplies. These ships where well known in the area since our entire empire depended on their sailing from the south county where grain was plentiful. These ships of Egyptian origin were strong and capable but were not designed for long open sea sailing, so our hope was to glide along the north shores, around the tip of Achaia and into the safer waters of Italia. As fate would have it, this was not to be. If I thought we had encountered contrary winds earlier in the week, what was about to blow over us in the few weeks ahead would be nothing short of a small hurricane!

Leaving Myra, attempting to continue west, we were met immediately with the same contrary wind opposing us. After sailing many days with great difficulty as far as the Cnidus Peninsula and not being able to approach the city for portage, we were forced to give in to the wind and sail south and under the Island of Crete just off of the city port of Salmone. At this juncture the wind became even more intense and opposing, threatening to push us ever closer into the open sea to the south. With yet more difficulty, we drove and propelled our modest ship under the eastern tip of Crete and dove directly to safety in a place called Fair Havens near the city of Lasea. Even with our ship safely in port, the strong winds and occasional rain storms buffeted the small bay and made staying longer a serious trial of patience.

It was here I made a most regrettable decision. Bringing the captain, the owner of the ship and several crew members together, I discussed the options. There were three at this stage of the voyage. We could stay here for the winter and put back to sea in about three or four months; we could attempt to push to the north on the edge of the open sea and try to make it to the southern tip of Greece where we might find more favorable winds; or we could make a quick run up the coast to the more suitable port of Phoenix and over-winter there. As the discussion was developing and opinions were being exchanged, the pressure of our lost time became obvious to us all. If a decision was to be made in favor of continuing, it needed to be made now. We simply did not have the luxury of wasting any more time. It was at this point that the prisoner Paul stepped into the conversation from somewhere in the hold of the ship. I had not seen him for several days since he had been preoccupied with his religious habits of fasting and prayer. So I was surprised to see him up on deck and a bit taken back at his boldness to approach us, given his chains. But, it was from this breaking of the fast that Paul approached us with a somber warning. 'Men', he said, 'I can see that this voyage is headed directly toward damage, heavy loss and possibly loss of our very lives', he continued, 'In my opinion, staying here is our safest option', he concluded.

The captain and the owner, being overly sensitive to their need to deliver cargo and also not wanting to winter where it would be unsafe for their ship, insisted that effort be made to get to Phoenix and there spend the rest of the winter. I was not sure of how much stock to put in the prisoner Paul's warning, seeing that he had little experience in these kind of matters, so, although a bit reluctant, I agreed that we should make the attempt to sail the half day trip into Phoenix. What should have been a simple half day trip turned out to a night mare of a journey and made me wish many times over that I had listened to Paul.

On the morning that we were ready to sail a gentle south wind sprang up from across the bay and we were certain that our fortunes had changed, so we weighed anchor, set the sail, turned the rudder and headed out along the shore of Crete toward the west. It appeared that this was exactly what we wanted and needed to reach the more secure harbor of Phoenix. Our hopes were short lived, however. As we progressed, inching our way up the coast, suddenly a strong 'northeaster' rushed down from the steep slopes of the island and struck us broadside. The island of Crete possessed many majestic mountains and massively rugged and jagged peaks and although beautiful to behold, they could become savage in their ability to promote typhoon like winds and weather along the coast. It was just one such blast that had now trapped us.

We were trapped in the grip of a snarling wind. As the 'northeaster' had pushed from the mainland up and over the high peaks of the island of Crete, the fierce pressure had created a firm funnel effect that was driving us out to the open sea. Our last chance of making land fall safely was soon passing by us on the right, in the form of the small island of Cauda. We helplessly watched as it sped by us and offered no help for our panic stricken craft. Our only option now was to give way to the wind and let the ship ride with the waves as the blustery coiling force drove us out to sea. It was at this juncture that we decided to pull the skiff aboard. It had been faithfully trailing behind us at the end of a long tether for all these weeks in case we needed to abandon ship. Since that was now a distinct possibility, we elected to keep it tied to the top deck. With much labor and struggle we were barely able to bring the small craft onto the deck and then with every ounce of strength that was left, we began using ropes and tackle to gird the ship's timbers, planks and cargo, which would help stabilize the vessel.

No sooner had we secured the skiff, but a fear of running aground swept over the captain and crew. Nothing brought fear like the possibility of being pounded into a sand bar and having the ship turn into an open target for the howling wind. In that kind of sandy death trap, the ship would break into a thousand pieces. To help prevent this, a large drift anchor was dropped off the stern to help hold us back against the driving wind and current.

Hour after hour we were being mercilessly and severely battered by the storm. It was decided later in the day, after the battering became almost unbearable, that some of the heavier cargo had to go. We began to jettison piece after piece of cargo, hoping to lighten the load and increase our chances of saving the ship. On the third day of our ordeal we had no choice but to begin throwing the ships gear overboard as well, since it added up to much of the weight of the ship. Painstakingly, the crew, amidst crashing waves and jarring wind blasts, disassembled the hoist mounts, the boom arms, the pulley supports, the extra mast and sail sheeting. It all went overboard. The days had turned to weeks and at this point in the torment, we had not seen the sun by day or the stars by night during any of this time. We were just driven along in a misty grey darkness that seemed to wrap all around us.

After nearly two weeks of this torture, it appeared that all was lost. I regretted daily my decision to attempt the trip in the first place. All on board were either exhausted, sick, frightened to the point of despair or all of these things combined. A sullen misery and hopelessness stood watch over every soul. It was expected at any moment that we would be tossed into the sea to be lost forever! In the middle of this plague of despondency, when several of us were trying to make a final assessment of our plight, we were approached by the prisoner from Judea. I'm not sure what I was expecting him to add to our conversation so when he started by pointing out to us our mistake in leaving Fair Haven, I was not impressed. I certainly agreed with him at this point, but all of that seemed of little use now. It was what he said next that caught me off guard and turned my head in disbelief.

"Men," Paul said, "I urge you to take courage, because there will be no loss of any of your lives, but only of the ship. For this night an angel of the God I belong to and serve stood by me and said: 'Paul, Don't be afraid!' You must stand before Caesar.' And, look indeed the Lord has graciously given you all those who are sailing with you." We were staring blankly at Paul, not really comprehending his words as he continued with boldness, "Therefore, take courage all of you men, because I believe God that it will be just the way it was conveyed to me. However, I must warn you that we will need to run aground on an island!"

I could not believe my ears! This Paul of the Hebrews had seen an angel who had promised us our lives! The God of Israel had decided to be gracious to us all and keep us alive? Those around me made little reaction to this declaration, largely because we were all completely out of strength and tired to the bone. But, of course, given the complete lack of other options we were very inclined to believe any such word that gave us even a shred of hope, so we listened intently as the instructions were rehearsed among us.

As we were approaching our fourteenth day of drifting and being driven by the wind in the Adriatic Sea, several of the sailors thought we were approaching land. The sound of the wind and the waves seemed to take on a different sound throughout the early evening with the distant reverberation of surf coming over the surface of the water to greet us. With this new development, the sailors scrambled to take a sounding of the water depth and found it to be 120 feet deep. This in itself told us that we were not in the open sea now, but moving over shallower waters. It would be the next sounding that would determine whether or not we were moving closer to land or farther away from it. After sailing a little farther along, the second sounding was made and they found it to be 90 feet. We had lost about 30 feet of depth over just a few minutes time. This indeed meant that we were about to be blown directly into some type of land mass. We could only hope that it wasn't some rocky place that would tear the bottom from the ship and leave us swimming for our lives!

Hoping to prevent a meeting with rock and waves, the order went out to drop anchors from the stern of the ship. Four huge lead anchors were lowered into the spraying waves and water, out the wide back of the ship over the top of the rudder. This, we hoped, would somehow slow our progress and keep us from being hurled forward against the island which we were sure was fast approaching. As the anchors and ropes disappeared behind us, we settled our mind and hearts as much as we could, praying and waiting for daylight to break.

It was several hours into our waiting that I was alerted to a commotion on the starboard side of the ship. Moving quickly to the side of the craft, with sword in hand, I caught sight of several sailors trying to lower the rescue skiff into the sea in order to make an attempt at escaping. Apparently these sailors had pretended to be throwing addition anchors off the bow in order to rush to the skiff to try and get it overboard. The noise of the turmoil brought soldiers and others to the deck to see what was happening. Immediately Paul called to me and several soldiers standing with me, 'Unless these men stay in the ship they cannot be saved!' Then, with lightning fast reaction, three soldiers dashed to the edge of the ship through the driven rain and, drawing their swords, slashed at the ropes holding the skiff to its mooring. The skiff slid along the decking and banged it way over the side of the rail and dropped silently into the raging sea below. There was no escaping now. Either Paul's God came through or we were doomed to the mercy of a deadly storm.

Daybreak did finally come and with that, Paul stood again to address us all, urging us to take some food in order to have enough strength to survive the rest of our ordeal. Reaching for his own bread and taking several bites, he gave thanks to his God in front of us all, assuring each of us that not a hair of our heads would be lost! This was indeed a heartening sign to behold. Paul's confidence seemed to bolster all of our resolve, soldier, prisoner and sailor alike. All 276 of us in the ship began to eat what was left of our rations. As strength slowly returned to both body and mind, it seemed that one last thing could be done to further lighten the ship for its final pitch toward shore. So with one last effort we all began to send container after container of grain into the salty expanse that surrounded us.

As more of the daylight spread over us and opened some of the clouds above us, in the distance was revealed a land mass directly off our bow. We were traveling in a direct path toward its shore, being pushed and pummeled by the nagging wind and spray of the fierce storm. The land was not recognizable nor was any other familiar landmark visible, but there did appear to be a small beach that might afford us a chance at a direct run up on the sand. With that, the four anchors were cut loose and left in the sea behind us and the ropes that held the rudders were loosened. Then the foresail was hoisted into the wind and, with a mighty jerk, the ship lurched forward toward the beach.

All of us could do nothing but watch. The foresail strained with the full force of the wind in it spread. The water crashed and slapped at all sides of the ship sending giant finger-like waves coursing across and over the deck. We watched and waited and held on for our very lives. Suddenly we were all thrown forward in the hold and along the railing. We had struck a sandbar and the ship was jammed fast into the hidden wall of sand and was not moving. In the moments after this reality settled on us, we were shaken again by several explosive thundering breakers that came slamming into the stern of the ship. Again they came crashing into and over the high stern section. As the pounding continued, the planks, decking, back railing and joists began their inevitable dismemberment and the entire stern of the ship began dropping piece by piece into the water. There was now no other choice but to abandon ship and throw ourselves into the sea.

As was standard procedure in emergencies like these, several of the soldiers began drawing their swords to kill the prisoners, lest they swim to shore and escape. But given the ordeal of the last three weeks and the presence of Paul, I could not bear to see this happen. Thus, I yelled at the top of my lungs, "Stay the sword!" Looking quickly out over the faltering dying vessel, I ordered all who could swim to jump over board and make for shore and for the others who could not swim to grab planking or debris from the ship and float their way to the beach. At that command, people began jumping, diving and dropping into the cold salty sea. From every direction individuals were entering the water around the ship, some splashing franticly as they began to swim, others desperately clutching debris or ship pieces to stay afloat. Sailors who were accustomed to the sea quickly responded. Prisoners and soldiers on the other hand, were more trepid in their effort, but given the options, they too found their way into the water and headed toward shore.

This entire frantic action was taking place as the vessel repeatedly shook from the continual pounding of the waves and huge breakers reaching high in the air, crashing and rolling over the deck. Dim shadowy figures could be seen fighting their way through the force of the spray and wind to get to the ship's side, over the railing, into the water and as far away from the stricken vessel as possible. At last, with most of the crew and passengers on their way, I climbed over a side rail, held myself out over the watery deep , took one last look back at the crumbling remains of the ship and then releasing my grip on the rail plunged into the sea. The cold shock of hitting the water sent my heart and mind reeling as I fervently flailed both arms forward to make headway toward the shore. Through the spray and waves that were washing over my back, head and face and over the bobbing pieces of debris, I could just make out in the distance a slender slice of a sandy beach and thus, with all my might, I headed for it. Rolling in the waves, spitting out water that attempted to fill my mouth and dragging drenched, heavy clothing and weaponry, I plowed through the white and grey water, all the while hearing Paul's words echoing in my mind, 'not a hair on your head will be lost'.

Making one's way through bubbling, frothing, boiling surf is no easy task. As I struggled forward against the waves, I wondered about the others. Were they making it onto the beach? What of my soldiers? Would the promise of this Paul of Tarsus hold them afloat amidst these crushing breakers? What of the prisoners, including Paul himself? How were they to find their way through this surging water with arm and leg wounds still fresh from the constant chafing of their previous chains? Some perhaps still in chains! Alas, there was not time to dwell on the others; I had to make my survival the priority for the time being.

Finally, after what seemed a very long and arduous time, I felt the rubbing of sand and pebbles moving under my feet. What a sense of relief and hope simultaneously flooded my mind as first one foot, then the other, found firm support under the rolling white topped waves. I staggered up the gradual slope of the beach as I found my footing and, with the help of both arms and hands, crawled and lurched out of the sea. This so called Apostle Paul had been right, at least for me. Although cold, bruised and disoriented, I was safe on the beach given another chance at life!

Kneeling in the soft wet sand and feeling the rhythmic slaps and blows of the waves from behind, I turned to see what was happening around me. Back over my right shoulder I could make out the twisted remains of the ship. It was still forged into the sand bar and being beaten and broken by huge breaking waves, each one sending powerful tremors through the remaining timbers and deck supports of the ships stern. I was sure from the towering size of the waves and the cracking sounds that blasted toward me that it would not be long before nothing would be left.

As I watched the ship in the distance, I could see in the foreground, all along the shoreline, small splashes and tiny staggering figures struggling up out of the surf, like so many creatures coming up out of their graves. Soldiers, sailors and prisoners strung out all along the beach line were crawling their way to safety and a future. Indeed, as I quickly counted those within my view, I had to conclude that the majority of the passengers, if not all of them, may have survived! A sudden burst of gratitude swept over my soul at that moment, as well as a gentle piercing jab of conviction, as the validity of Paul's words came into focus in my mind. This God, to whom Paul belonged and served, had chosen to rescue all of us out of the most extreme of circumstances, a harrowing brush with death and a crucial lapse in common sense.

Walking slowly up the sandy beach, I was eventually joined by the other survivors, who, one by one, checked in. With each additional person stepping forward, I realized, as I had done earlier, that ALL on board had survived and would live to tell our story. As the crowd grew larger and all of us at once were reciting our individual ordeals, the topics of conversation turned toward the one person that we all had on our minds and were looking for; this Paul of Tarsus.

With several inquiries called out over the gathering group, Paul finally made his way through the exhausted and emotionally spent passengers. Walking gently and deliberately around some who were kneeling, some who appeared to be praying, others who were flat on their face against the sand and still others who were softly crying in relief, Paul stepped alongside me, toward the center of our large uneven semi-circle of weary people.

As everyone became aware that Paul was standing before us, a quiet reverence prompted by deep respect settled over the entire group. Whether we were just too tired to talk, or the shock of our ordeal was still gripping us, or we were simply in awe of the gracious miracle we had just experienced, I was not sure. I only knew that no one wanted to speak. For several minutes we held our peace and cherished the moment. With the wind continuing, rain pelting us from all directions, the still present distant echoes of the surf devouring our ship; we quietly paid our respect to the God of Paul of Tarsus.

I am sure this hallowed moment would have continued for some time longer had our concentration not been interrupted by the sounds of voices and commotion coming to us from the tree line above the beach. A few quick glimpses and we realized that not only were we all alive on an unfamiliar but safe beach, but we were also being greeted and welcomed by the inhabitants of the island. They were carrying torches and preparing to start several fires on the beach by which we could warm ourselves. This was almost a dreamlike conclusion to a horrifying three week voyage to the brink of death and back. All of which would become a lasting testimony to a humble and wrongly accused man and the personal care and power of his God!

DOUGLAS S. MALOTT

CHAPTER EIGHT:
THE TRIUMPHAL ENTRY AND CRUCIFIXION OF JESUS
MATTHEW 21:16-44; MATTHEW 27:30-60

Historical background and setting

The year is approximately 25-30 A.D. The teacher and prophet, Jesus of Nazareth, is about to make his final entry into Jerusalem, after about 3 and ½ years of public ministry. This entry is what we have traditional called the 'Triumphal Entry' and the beginning of the 'Passion Week' of Jesus. During this time he would be falsely accused, arrested, tried under questionable circumstances and eventually crucified by the Romans with full cooperation of the Jewish religious leaders. An unnamed Roman Centurion would be given charge of this gruesome duty and thus witness the entire crucifixion scenario.

The Story

I am a Roman Centurion, stationed in Judea and assigned by the Roman government the duty of general peacekeeping, maintaining law and order and supervising all crucifixions. One particular episode on the crucifixion hill of Golgotha, just outside the ancient walled City of Jerusalem, was for me no usual execution. It involved a so called Jewish itinerate prophet from Galilee and was to be a straight forward punishment of a convicted malcontent. As I would soon realize it turned out to something very different. In fact, it was an execution like no other I had ever witnessed and as such, would begin a slow but dramatic change in my life from that point forward. This is my story.

This Jesus of Nazareth had arrived in Jerusalem earlier in the festival week with a grand and dramatic entrance that some said was the arrival of a Jewish King. In those days leading up to the Passover Feast several units of foot soldiers, under my command, were given the task of making careful watch over the crowd entering and leaving the City of Jerusalem. With the increase in traffic coming in from many regions beyond Jerusalem we had been warned of possible insurgent activity from some who wanted to embarrass Rome during the Jewish feast days. So, with this threat in the back of my mind, I emptied the Antonia Fortress of every possible soldier and stationed groups of them throughout the city of Jerusalem to pay close attention to all entry points. It was my hope that from these strategic positions on and around its walls, we could adequately observe activity in the surrounding areas. So...the commencement and progress of this 'unofficial' royal welcome of the supposed Jewish King was seen firsthand by me and several of my foot soldiers. It was those assigned to the Shushan Gate, which was the primary entry point on the city's eastern wall, who saw this entry first hand.

To the east and south of this section of the city, beyond the quiet Garden of Gethsemane, lay two small settlements, Bethphage and Bethany. These were quaint but primitive villages located just beyond the crest of the Mount of Olives on the road to Jericho that coils and curls away from Jerusalem. It was from these wayside hamlets that this Jesus of Nazareth had begun his journey into Jerusalem.

The point where we were first able to see him was at the brink of the Mt. Olive hill as it came sloping downward into the Kidron Valley, just below our vantage point.

Perched on the crest of the hill we could see the growing throng of people surrounding him there. He was sitting on a small beast of burden, a donkey, as I recall, and surrounded by his disciples.

Attending this group were several concerned priests, groups of excited followers and of course the curious. All of these who walked beside him were preparing to descend toward us and the city.

It was clear to us that the people in the city and those milling and waiting below along the wall had recognized him and were forming an additional welcome at the point where he approached the gate. In fact many had begun running up the road in hopes of meeting him and his processional at the mid-way point. Branches from the scattered Palm trees in the area had been plucked by many who intended to wave them in honor of the arrival of this Jesus. The sudden burst of scattered activity across the valley told us these people were expecting someone of importance. We only hoped the welcome would be peaceful and short lived.

Watching with guarded optimism, we noticed that what should have been a deliberate and very easy descent to the valley floor had stalled at the crown of the hill. The cheering, laughing voices, which we had heard for some time now from the crowds, had quieted and now a more somber tone prevailed with the notice of this unexpected stoppage.

From our vantage point along the top of Jerusalem's wall looking east, the distant figure on the donkey appeared to have stopped in order to gaze out over the city. He was gazing, in fact, in our direction.

Thinking back later over this peculiar development I realized that all of those on the hill top would have had a grand and panoramic view of the entire eastern side of the city. From their elevated angle the whole of the majestic and grand Hebrew temple, its courts and its dominance over the landscape would have been in full view.

Was this man, who later would be arrested, looking at something in particular? Did the Temple capture his view? Did he have some special attachment to this historical relic? Or, was the city itself, now ablaze in glorious sunshine and light, arresting his attention? Was his gaze one of longing or inspiration or retribution? Was the stoppage simply planned to enable more people to gather or perhaps to have more momentum build before his actual entry? I could not tell!

I now wonder if this prophet from Galilee was not seeing in his mind's eye the day when this majestic and imposing city along with its regal and stately temple would be leveled to the ground and destroyed. It would be so completely destroyed in fact, that not a single stone would be left upon another. We, of course, could not really tell his true motivation from where we were observing the whole scene, it just simply seemed curious to us all. Several of my soldier companions were even sure that they saw this mysterious figure weeping as he remained perched atop the donkey. They were certain they could see his head bowed for a time and his mantle draped shoulders shake with anguish while several around him attempted to steady his mount.

This was no kingly entry that I had ever seen. Most were prominent and grandiose, staged perfectly to show strength, power and authority to the watching masses. Any emperor, king, governor or high political figure I had ever seen wanted to impress his followers, inspire his armies and strike fear in the heart of this enemies. This was not the case here. This suspected insurrectionist and possible messiah king was coming in tears and simplicity; in my mind a most puzzling approach.

Soon the procession continued winding its way down the well traveled and dusty road into the valley below, picking up many more groups of sympathetic onlookers as it moved along. All of these additional people were likewise standing ready with wild anticipation of his coming.

Now that the large mass of people was approaching the gate, spontaneous shouts of praise could be heard echoing overhead and reverberating against the massive stone walls of the city. It seemed at times the whole valley rang with these expressions, praise and joy alternating from wall to hill, back and forth, across the valley. Blankets and robes were being thrown to the ground in front of him to make an official pathway for his donkey to travel.

As the procession neared the north east corner of the city wall and then made a sharp southerly turn to enter the gate, many more of the temple priests joined the throng of greeters, given now the close proximity of the Temple Complex. Many of these priests, being very unhappy at the proclamations of the crowd, demanded that he stop them from saying such blasphemous things. His response - He did not stop them! He strangely replied to their demands that if these people did not speak out then the very rocks would need to do so!

Making the final passage under the arched top of the Shushan gate structure, the crowd spread slightly allowing the donkey rider to dismount and make his way up the broad steps of the Temple Complex and through the Gate Beautiful into the Temple's courtyard. Everyone seemed to be following after him at this point to see what might happen next. From our strategic position nothing sinister or illegal had taken place and thus we saw no reason to intervene or interrupt the proceeding. Even with the emotions and anger on the part of the Jewish religious leaders, it all seemed harmless to us. In spite of the rumors that came later, about a plot by the chief priest and scribes to eliminate this man, it had been just another day in the life of a Roman centurion serving in a city where strange religious activities and commotions were the usual fair.

Over the next couple of days business for those of us charged with keeping the peace was mostly what was to be expected. Only late in the week did we receive official word that an upheaval may be in the making and two events at the beginning of the week made this rumor clearly plausible.

This Jesus of Nazareth, I was told, had apparently spent the week moving in and out of the city and maneuvering his presence among the people to purposely confront the Chief Priests and Elders.

First of all, it was reported by reliable sources that later on the very day of his royal entry into Jerusalem, he had gone directly into the Temple's outer Court of the Gentiles and proceeded to disrupt the money changers and sacrifice providers. This was no small disruption I was told! As he had ascended the main stairs up into the complex, this Jesus had gone directly across the open court to the long row of tables and booths piled high with money boxes and loose coins.

Taking only a fleeting moment to assess the situation, he had made his way suddenly parallel to the vendors, lifting and upending table after table, sending money, supplies and angry merchants in every direction. As tables fell sideways and awkwardly skittered against the stone floor, thousands of coins rolled and bounced along with them on the rock making a cacophony of pinging tinkling sounds. Not being finished with his assault, he had continued his attack by setting loose scores of animals and birds waiting to be purchased for sacrifice. As people and animals ran in every direction, the confusion was extreme and the consternation on the faces of the priests was blatant, I was told.

Secondly, only one day after his thrust against the marketing section of the courtyard, he had directly confronted the chief priests with a barrage of condemnations and insults. This Jesus, although carefully upholding the honor of the House of God and the sacredness of the Law, had pointed out with glaring clarity the corruption of the sacrificial system and the deception of the Jewish religious leaders. Apparently, in no uncertain words, he had exposed their hypocrisy and called them all 'whitened sepultures'; clean on the outside but full of death. It was not surprising that a fierce debate and emotional inferno eventually took place in the Jewish courts.

Because of these events in the temple, the unrest in Jerusalem was now building to a higher level than was usual.

And to add to the turmoil the Governor, Pontius Pilate, had been brought a man accused by the Jewish authorities of being guilty of blasphemy; the highest order of infraction possible in the Hebrew courts. It did not surprise me really to find out that this man was the same Jesus of Nazareth that we had watched receive such a hardy welcome earlier in the week.

And with the temple attack, along with the public disgrace he handed to the Jewish leaders, it followed logically to me that they would find a way to accuse this man of blasphemy; can you imagine it, actually claiming to be God? In the mind of the Sanhedrin leaders, this offense was worthy of death and with witnesses claiming to have heard him make such statements, along with a supposed self confession, they had been insistent that this Jesus be put to death.

However, since Rome did not allow capital punishment to be carried out unless sanctioned and supervised by its own authorities, the High Priest and elders had tried this man, found him guilty and had then brought him to Pilate for examination and hopefully for sentencing.

I had been on duty in the Governor's palace for some of these early conversations and knew that the Governor was not convinced that this Jesus of Nazareth was really guilty of anything, let alone blasphemy. And, even if it were somehow proven according to Jewish law that this was true, he did not believe him worthy of death. It seemed to me that my illustrious leader was stuck in a most serious political trap. On the one hand he wanted to keep peace in Jerusalem and the region beyond and this was best done by cooperating with the Jewish leaders and turning this man over to be executed.

On the other hand, he was not agreeable to simply signing off on these kinds of requests when he knew full well the motivation behind the appeal. It was nothing but a veiled attempt at protecting their authority and prestige. He was not really sure if this Jesus was guilty, but what he did know was that the Jewish leaders wanted to get rid of him.

Well, in due process of time, the trials and

examinations brought Pilate to his final decision. Even after having this Jesus mercilessly flogged and beaten, he saw that this did not detour the leaders in their anger, even in the slightest. So, needing to maintain his working relationship with these leading priests, this Jesus of Nazareth, assumed messiah by many and accused rebel by the Sanhedrin, was sentenced to be crucified. And, as it turned out, I would be the one to see to it that the crucifixion was carried out with efficiency and the least amount of disturbance.

Being a centurion meant that the 80 to 100 or so soldiers under my care and authority would need to assist me in the process of bringing this criminal, and perhaps others, to the place of death; Golgotha's hill. It was on this small hill just outside the northwest portion of the city wall, between the Fish gate and the Gennath gate, that executions were routinely performed. This location, between the two gates, afforded a very visible deterrent to crime for the residents of Jerusalem who would travel this route regularly and thus see dying and suffering criminals just outside their city. It was to this place that I would be taking Jesus of Nazareth for his final hours of life. And as fate would have it, this would be done at the beginning of the Jewish festival of Passover, when thousands of Jewish pilgrims would travel to Jerusalem. All of these pilgrims were coming to their fair city to visit the great temple and be present when the entire nation would kill their Passover lamb and eat their Passover meal together.

From the Praetorium where Pilate pronounced his final verdict, the prisoner would need to be taken a short half mile to the crucifixion site. This was normally an uneventful walk, with a few onlookers and a few of the curious watching the procession. The guilty would be taken to the outer court area and prepared for the walk. Tradition and law stated that the guilty would carry their own death sentence in the form of a portion of their cross. Thus, they were tied to the cross beam of their own cross and made to carry it to the execution area. But, the turmoil in the city due to the recent activities of this Jesus and the fomented rage on the part of the Jewish leaders had aroused great interest and passion among the people.

Getting this prisoner and two others with him along the narrow pathways and streets would require extreme patience and high security. We did not want either detractors or supporters to make a scene; neither did we want some fanatical sect in the city to attempt either a rescue or an assassination! So we were on high alert, dressed in full armor and ready for whatever might happen as we left Pontius Pilate's judgment seat and made our way to the place of the skull.

What complicated the matter of traversing the short distance through this corner of the city was the fact that this Jesus had been beaten so severely that he could hardly walk. Still bloodied and faint from his flogging he struggled to even maintain his balance. Fresh blood still oozed from his punctured scalp down into his eyes over his face making it nearly impossible to see his way over the cobbled street. After moving just a few labored steps out into the street our prisoner stumbled and fell under the weight of his cross beam.

Several attempts, with whip and rod, at making him stand upright and continue on were unsuccessful, even at the threat of additional beatings he could not precede. Our only choice was to subscribe one of the onlookers who seemed in support of this supposed savior. Quickly and without explanation a man in the crowd was dragged into the street, stripped of his belongings and given the cross beam that Jesus of Nazareth had been carrying. Together he and the faltering man from Galilee continued the agonizing walk through the narrow streets to Golgotha.

Once at the site, three crosses were prepared for their victims. Large and long wood beams were laid on the ground, each in excess of fifteen feet in length. After each criminal's cross beam had been cut loose, the prisoners were forced to knee in a huddle together where wine and gall were given to them in a disguised attempt at deadening their senses toward the torture that was about to take place. The two thieves who would be crucified with this Jesus each took their drinks and quickly swallowed hard. This Jesus, however, refused his portion.

Now, the cross beams were lifted and placed on the three matching wood poles, perpendicular to the main beam. These were secured and readied for each of the prisoners, who was stripped down to his loin cloth and forced to make one of the crosses his tortured bed. Laying parallel on the center beam, their arms were extended one to the left, the other to the right and then with several swift, jarring slams of the hammer, crude iron nails were thrush through each wrist into the wood surface behind.

At this point in the process, and I had seen this happen over and over again in previous settings, those being crucified would begin to scream in agony and hope for some kind of mercy to be shown them. The two thieves did exactly that, but this Jesus, though in excruciated pain and twisted grimacing, did not make a cry for mercy nor did he scream out in pain. This was just one more peculiar thing about this man that should have alerted me to his unearthly manner and quality, but I did not see it.

Being in charge of the proceedings put me a short distance from the action while my subordinates carried out the gruesome details of finalizing the executions. Watching intently I marked in my mind the next steps taken to complete the crucifixion. After arms and wrists were spiked to the beams, additional support was added by wrapping rope several times around each arm and beam.

Then, each man's feet, one foot on the other were secured. This was done by, once again, taking another large iron nail spike and with several hard hammer blows driving it through the flesh and bone into the bottom extension of the beam. With all three men secured to their crosses, writhing in pain and looking from their ground level view into the sky, each of the crosses was lifted slowly by rope and pulley into the air.

As the impaled men dangled momentarily on their crosses over the ground, an appointed soldier ran quickly to guide the bottom of each beam into the ground hole designed to hold them. As the hole and beam were brought into alignment, the ropes were dropped, sending the pulleys into a wild spin and jamming each cross firmly down in the rock and earth. As the beams slid and jolted abruptly into place, each one of the suffering men was jerked and wrenched on his wooden frame, only increasing his anguish and torment.

Now the guilty were simply left to twist between the nails, push from their throbbing ankles and crane their neck and shoulders in useless effort to gasp for air. Their torturous suffocation would be slow and possibly take the rest of the evening and night to complete; some had been known to take more than one day to finally die.

As was usual at this point, the guards assigned to the actual crucifixion detail sorted through the few clothes and belongings left by the hanging victims. In most cases the whole assortment of items were either divided and taken or simply burned. In the case of this Jesus, however, his garment, an unusual unstitched and seamless woven robe, was gambled over, with the winner taking the treasure by the casting of lots. Now all that was left to do was wait, wait until the slow agony of suffering brought on death.

To pass my time I mounted my horse, with its circular side-mounted shield and my long stave easily accessible just in case it was needed to push or prod people who might get too close. Looking up the slight incline to the very top of Golgotha's hill, I could clearly see the three crosses silhouetted against the clear sky and high noon sun. A blasphemer and two thieves side by side, suspended between heaven and earth, alone and largely unknown, except for the dying Galilean, whose beam marker stated simply: THIS IS JESUS THE KING OF THE JEWS.

Scattered along the crest of the hill and along both pathways which led up and down the hill, people stood looking and gawking. Some were crying, some were yelling insults and throwing small stones, while others stood mocking the one from Nazareth and daring him to come off his cross to save himself. Several groups of priests stood watching and discussing among themselves their final victory over this figure on the center cross while mocking him as well.

Then, as the sun over head passed its mid-position, a strange and frightening thing began to develop. At the highest point of the day when the sun was to be at its brightest and hottest, the entire sky as far I could see in all directions began to darken. A sinister gray heaven spread overhead, displacing the sun little by little and giving the effect of an early night. I was startled and could feel the unease in my steed under me. We both sensed an unusual and mysterious warning in the atmosphere. Something was changing in the air. All of the people who still were loitering over the hill location began to react as well. Some pointed upward and cried out their concern. Others became agitated as if seeing some omen or sign from heaven opening before them and quickly began making their way down the pathway. This hovering dark sky remained entrenched for almost three hours and as it turned out; its appearance and deepening horror seemed to progress as this Jesus of Nazareth was slowly drained of life.

As I watched this phenomenon, I could not help but think that heaven was watching this crucifixion and responding to the death of this mysterious figure on the center cross! It was as if the very environment reacted and was repulsed at his loss of life, reversing its own progression as the Galilean drifted toward death! When we reached the close of the noon watch, at about 3 o'clock, the Nazarene suddenly cried out in a loud and painful voice, 'My God, my God, why have you forsaken me?'

As these lasts words left his lips a cold shiver passed over my shoulders and neck. A chill crept up my spine and suddenly my pulse quickened. Was this man crying out to God in his final moments of life? Was he more than what these religious leader thought or wanted him to be?

At one point, one of the onlookers ran to retrieve a long reed, placed a sponge saturated with sour wine on its tip and attempted to hold the concoction high enough to enable the Nazarene to drink. I suppose he was thinking that the man needed a swig of distraction from his pain. Some thought he was calling for Elijah the prophet and hoping in fact, that Elijah would indeed come.

Still others only continued to mock his cries and seemed, by their defiant tone, to dare Elijah to appear. I only hoped that his death would come soon and this troubling darkened day would return to normal.

With almost three hours now spent since the victims were lifted to the sky for their pathetic death, the two thieves hung writhing on their crosses, one crying and one cursing as they fought to find breath to even speak. This Jesus, however, remained mostly silent. Finally and abruptly he gave out one final cry of pain, anguish and relief and was dead.

I was indeed relieved myself and for a very short moment let down my guard with a sigh, only to be rudely startled by the ground shaking beneath me. My horse reared up slightly at the odd sensation of being jostled from below. People everywhere on the hill scattered, being terrified of this new development. Boulders that had sat loosely on the ground turned or shifted and some rolled with the sway of the earth. All three crosses teetered with the earth's convulsions. In the distance behind us the western wall of the city seemed to shutter as well. Not only had the heavens recoiled at the suffering of this man but the very earth that supported his cross seemed to be in rebellion to his death! For several minutes we were caught helpless on the trembling surface of the earth only to hope that it did not include us in the pall of death that now was surrounding us.

Later in the night after the upheaval had passed, numerous rumors and stories would filter my way. Apparently some in the city would see ghosts or mysterious images of past dead saints or relatives appearing to them and the appearances would continue through the ongoing days of the Passover. As well as this, several of the Hebrew priests assigned to the temple's daily duties and rituals would report being traumatized beyond words by a most shocking sight. What was described as a massive angelic being materialized and stood behind and over the 60 foot temple veil that marked the entrance to the inner sanctum. Leaning over it and taking hold of the top rail with his cosmic hands, he tore the veil completely in two from top to bottom! Given the peculiar accouterments of the earlier crucifixion I was inclined to believe these reports and wondered what the chief leaders of the Sanhedrin thought of this man now!

The earthquake had now sent most people scattering for their lives, with the exception of my fellow guards and soldiers, who along with me were terrified at what was happening around them, but could not leave their appointed tasks and posts. What I was seeing troubled me deeply!

The unusual humble demeanor of this supposed criminal, the frightening hours of unlikely blackness that paced his lost of life and now the earthquake that coincided with his last breath injected a wave of conviction and awe into my heart. As the quake began to subside and the sky cleared slowing, I had but one conclusion, 'This man really was God's son!', and his death had not been taken lightly by the forces of heaven!

Among those brave ones who elected to stay put during the drama of the Galilean's death were many women who had followed this man from Galilee and had invested their time, energy and substance to serve him. These, in their sorrowful and tearful state, stood leaning together, braced against the blackness and shaking earth, still watching him from a distance. This Jesus was dead and gone but they in their love and devotion for him lingered and mourned.

In the stillness that finally returned to the hill, only the low shallow groans of the two crucified thieves could be heard. Although I wished with every fiber of my being to leave this scene, I could not; my duty required that I remain, along with my entire troop assignment, until the victims were all confirmed to be dead. If the agony of their dying was prolonged, we were instructed to take two final steps to insure that death came. First, we attempted to break each one's legs, essentially stopping their reflexive effort to push their body upward while gasping for air. This would quickly complete the suffocation process. Along with this measure, a sword was plunged upward into the victim's side to pierce the heart and lungs. One or both of these actions would accomplish our goal. Systematically the process was to be carried out for all three of the prisoners, but when the soldier detail approached this Jesus, only one of the actions was required for this one was already dead. To simply confirm this reality, his side was pierced and his hanging body then left alone. It was almost as if he had given up and entered his death willingly. The other two remained dying slowly and agonizingly in their places.

What had been a beehive of activity, emotion and suffering now became deathly in its silence. The stale aroma of drying blood and death hung in the air and only a gentle breeze could be felt drifting over the hill and valley. Still I waited into the early night hours for any who might claim the bodies of the deceased.

Sadly no one would end up coming for the thieves and we were then responsible for taking their twisted, contorted bodies from the crosses and finding some forgotten place to bury their remains. This was not so for the man on the middle cross. Soon numerous of his followers gathered at the foot of his cross and waited until I confirmed the official death notice and acknowledged the official receipt allowing the body to be taken.

Slowly and carefully the group was assisted by three soldiers in bringing the body off the cross to be wrapped and carried away. The women and a prominent man from the city gingerly wiped and cleaned the lifeless form as best as could be done in the dwindling light and ceremoniously placed a clean fine linen wrap around the body. With this done and daylight failing fast, I watched as this small group of devoted followers found their way down the narrow path and disappeared in the distance into a small private garden area where, no doubt, some tomb arraignments had been made ready.

Turning my gaze from the empty crosses and pulling slightly to the side on the reins of my horse, I pointed and nudged him into an exit trot. All the while I could not but think that if indeed this man was the son of God and the bizarre phenomenon of this long and trying evening were designed to confirm that fact, then was it not possible that the tomb he was about to enter could prove unable to hold him? That thought proved more than I could really comprehend at the moment. For now, tired and weary, I simply wanted to end my day and start a fresh one with the morning sunrise that would soon appear.

CHAPTER NINE:
ELIJAH AND THE PROPHETS OF BAAL
I KINGS 17/18

<u>Historical background and setting</u>

The year was approximate 874-853 B.C. The Nation of Israel had been divided for many years into 10 northern tribes of Israel and 2 southern tribes of Judah. The northern kingdom of Israel had been led by a succession of ungodly kings, of which King Ahab was one of the worst offenders, along with his wife Jezebel. During the reign of Ahab, the prophet Elijah was actively attempting to call the nation Israel back to the Lord. This tug of war between Elijah and Ahab culminated with a dramatic confrontation on Mt Carmel. In the court of Ahab was a humble servant of the King that continued to fear the Lord, amidst the advancing paganism, whose name is Obadiah. In this Mt. Carmel confrontation he is an eye witness.

The Story

My name is Obadiah, servant to the King of Israel and this is my story. I had long served the King of Israel and the people of Israel as a messenger and assistant to King Ahab and his queen Jezebel. The years of service were difficult and trying, to say the least, since my King did not walk in the ways of his father David, but turned his heart toward Baal and Asherah and led the people into idolatry under the sinister and menacing influence of his wife Jezebel. I had remained true to the fear of the Lord while honoring my King and earning his trust in many matters, attempting to faithfully serve the true God of Israel; possibly bringing influence to the King that would turn him back to his faith. This intention proved a very complicated matter, especially with the king and queen's distrust of Elijah, the Prophet of the Lord. King Ahab chose to be more tolerant toward the prophet than his queen. He avoided the prophet whenever possible and hoped that the fiery man of God would do the same for him. The queen Jezebel, on the other hand, hated the prophet and sought at every turn to destroy him!

At one point in this whole episode I was prompted by my own convictions and fear of the Lord to hide some 100 of his prophets in a cave deep in the hills while providing them with food and water. All because Jezebel, Israel's queen, was systematically slaughtering them whenever she found them, hoping somehow to get her hands on Elijah. She was only the more frustrated and infuriated when Elijah could not be caught and it appeared that the Lord Jehovah himself was committed to protecting him. This of course was fine with me. I did not want to be on the bad side of the prophet, nor did I want to see him eliminated. Our nation needed his word and his leadership in spite of the godlessness of our king and his wife.

At the point I begin this story, Israel had been on the tail end of three full years of draught. By the word of the Lord, Elijah had declared that the heavens would be shut for three years and the land would become a desolate wilderness of dust and sagebrush due to the nation's godlessness. It had indeed happened just as he had said and the whole of the nation suffered. This word of the Lord had come in response to the King's deliberate refusal to honor God and his failure to deal with his wife and her royal court. As the third year was drawing to an end, Elijah had come out of hiding to present himself to the king. The famine was severe in the whole land of Samaria and I had been sent to search for water and green foliage in every wadi, oasis, water source and distant hill side in hopes of keeping the King's horses and mules alive. The shortage of water was so severe that we feared the loss of our cattle and herds at any time.

The King had divided the land in half and instructed me to search one way while he searched the other way. We had made arrangements, gathered our supplies and started the grim task at the same time. I had not traveled many miles from the palace when suddenly I was confronted by a familiar figure. As my eyes focused and the mind gathered its thoughts, I realized that I was face to face with the great prophet himself. Wasting no time, I fell quickly to my knees and then to the ground with my face pressed firmly in the dust. Knowing full well who was before me, but fearing this man of God and his reputation, I humbly mumbled into the earth, "Is that you my lord Elijah?", to which he replied simply, "It is I, now stand to your feet and go tell your King that Elijah is here!".

I could not believe what I was hearing! He wanted me to report to the King that the great prophet was arriving! Had I sinned against God or the prophet to have this death sentence imposed upon me? Ahab had sent many of his servants into all corners of the land looking for this man of God and then killed them when they returned without him. Others who dared promise the prophet would come only to find out that he had no intentions of cooperating with this godless king were put to death on the spot. If Elijah was playing the same kind of tricks, then I was sure to be dead just like the rest! I envisioned in my mind reporting to the King of Elijah's location, only to have the Spirit of the Lord whisk him away before any of the King's soldiers could arrive to seize him and I would be executed instantly! No thanks, I told him! I did not want to be that messenger and since he knew I feared the Lord deeply, I was greatly disturbed by his inquiry. As I stood to my feet, trembling and twitching in fear, he simple looked me straight in the eye, reached his hand to my shoulder in reassurance and said flatly, "As the Lord of Host lives, before whom I stand, today I will present myself to Ahab." With those words he waited momentarily for me to turn back in the direction of the King and then began following me at a distance, giving me time to announce his arrival after I found King Ahab.

It was not long before these two quite opposite men met each other. King Ahab had no kind word for the prophet whom he blamed for the terrible waste conditions in the land. Elijah, as well, had no kind word for the King, for it was he and his father's house that had abandoned the Lord and caused the whole nation to follow Baal. From the fire and zeal in the prophet's eye I could see that a confrontation was imminent. And from what I knew of Elijah this would be no small thing. As Elijah turned to leave, he gave Ahab one last word of command, "Summon all of Israel to meet me at Mount Carmel and bring as well the 450 prophets of Baal and the 400 prophets of Asherah who now eat at Jezebel's table."

Mount Carmel was a regal mountain bluff on the west coast of Samaria at the south western end the Kishon valley. Its west side dropped abruptly some 1,500 feet to sea level and sat only a short distance from the sea itself. Its east facing side sloped gradually down to a level valley that bordered the central foothills of the northern Kingdom of Israel. Its top possessed a full view of the Great Sea which lay a bit further to the west and thus was a frequent destination for the roving prophet. Why exactly this location was chosen, I did not know. I only knew that the man of God had serious business on his mind and was not to be detoured. Perhaps this high place would provide a dramatic backdrop for a head to head clash of religions. While his final words hung in the air over the King's head, he turned his gaze westward, struck his rod firm to the ground and began moving in the direction of the mountain.

Immediately and nervously, King Ahab sprang to action. He began organizing couriers and messengers to be sent in every direction throughout the length and breadth of Samaria. The King was calling all the people to Mt. Carmel for a special summit with Elijah the Prophet of God and no one would want to miss this occasion. It appeared to me that the godlessness of the nation of Israel and the holiness of the God of Israel were being maneuvered for a clash of historical proportions. I wondered what might be the results; revival, restoration…rebellion, bloodshed? I hoped and prayed for the former and not the latter!

I, Obadiah, being in charge of the palace and the King's servants and helpers, arrived with the King and his entourage ahead of the great throng of people that were expected. I saw to it that the royal tent, throne and attendants were in their places, as people from every city and village arrived to watch the proceedings. Throughout the next several days people gathered, set up their make shift temporary housing and waited for the prophet to appear.

It was not long before he did arrive and proceeded to find a prominent spot overlooking the majority of the crowd. This, it appeared, was to be able to address them personally as the meeting was to begin. Standing on a grouping of boulders, which allow him to look out over the people; he motioned for their attention and then proceeded to speak. It was a challenge! Without hesitation, he struck at the hard heart of the nation, "How long will you hesitate between two opinions?" he now shouted. "If the Lord is God, follow Him! But if Baal is God, then follow him!" At the sound of these words, the people seemed shocked and mute. They had come to watch the proceedings, not be questioned about their loyalties! No one dared give an answer to the man of God. Elijah boldly continued, "I am the only remaining prophet of the LORD, but Baal's prophets number 450 men. Now I have a proposal, let two bulls be given to us. They, the prophets of Baal, are to choose one bull for themselves, cut it in pieces, and place it on the wood of an altar, but not light the fire. I will also prepare the other bull and place it on the wood of another altar and also, not light the fire. Then, those who serve as priests of Baal will call on the name of their god and I will call on the name of Yahweh. And the God who answers with fire, let him be God." At this the people became energized and responsive. They indeed agreed with the proposal and seemed eager to assist in the preparations!

For several minutes groups of men scavenged the area for boulders and rock that would meet the requirements for an altar. Once the collection of stone was assembled, several the priests of Baal carefully stacked and piled and maneuvered the stones to form the sacrificial altar. Another gathered sticks and wood from the area and placed them on top of the altar to provide kindling and fuel for the fire. One of the bulls that had been secured from among those who had gathered to watch, was killed, divided according to custom and the pieces, still dripping with fresh blood, were placed on the top the altar structure. The altar, its wood and its sacrifice now stood alone waiting for Baal's fire. As the crowd grew quiet, the prophets of Baal encircled the altar and began calling on their god. This first installment of the whole process began in the morning and went on for about 3 hours. "Baal, answer us", they called. "Baal, hear our cries", they screamed. But in the shouting and screaming there was no answer, no response, no sound, the prophets of Baal were left with nothing but an untouched altar and silence. At this point they began to dance and hobble and move rhythmically around the bloody pieces of bull on the altar, chanting and calling to their silent god.

At the noon hour, with the masses of people still curiously watching the bizarre ceremony, Elijah began mocking the feeble effort of his rivals. He called to them, "Shout more loudly! Maybe he is still thinking over your request, or maybe he has wandered away somewhere, or perhaps he is still on the road! It could be that he is still sleeping. Shout to wake him up", he called to them as they carried on their fruitless gyrations and movements. In their frustrations, they attempted to bring Baal into action by shouting louder. Soon, as was their regular custom, knives and spears began to appear and ritual cutting and stabbing took place through the entire gathering of these prophets. Man after man was now bleeding, drippings of blood could be seen on arms and legs and necks. Their heads, faces and hands ran red with the gushing, spurting, pulsing blood from their own bodies. Many in the multitude who were still gathered were repulsed by the scene and moved some distance away from the blood-spattered area. All of this went on unnoticed by the dazed, entranced priestly dancers. Throughout the entire afternoon, prophet after prophet would take his turn trying to arouse this Baal. But to no avail! Their ravings would produce nothing but silence. No sound, no answer; nothing was heard, Baal did not seem to pay attention!

After some time of watching their pathetic efforts, Elijah returned to his rocky perch in order to call the people still gathered. Motioning for them to come closer he called, "Come near, gather in closer!" Gingerly the throng pressed in toward the prophet, wondering what his intentions might be at this stage of the day. Pointing to a flat area, just to his right, he brought everyone's focus to a broken down pile of former altar stones. It became clear to me now as to why he had chosen this very location. It had once, in the former days of service to Jehovah, been an altar location dedicated to the God of Israel. It appeared from my vantage point that Elijah was about to rebuild it! And he was going to do so in full view of the entire assembled people of Israel.

With painstaking precision Elijah began gathering 12 large stones from the ruined heap. As each stone was retrieved, dusted off and set in place, Elijah would pronounce, "Israel will be your name!", and as each stone, one by one found its place, each the tribes of Israel were assigned to them. With the final stone in place and Yahweh's name pronounced over them, the prophet Elijah stepped back and gazed upon the work. There in the form of this restored altar of God, the whole nation of Israel was represented. At first glance one would have thought the prophet was done. He was not! With a large stick and his own hands he began to dig a trench around the altar at its bottom, where stone touched soil. It looked to be enough space to hold about 4 gallons of water. Next Elijah collected and arranged his own sticks and wood for the altars top, then killed the second bull and placed its severed bloody pieces on the wood where the fire would be ignited. Now the Altar of the Lord was ready with its wood and bloody sacrifice waiting for its fire!

It was at this point that the preparation took a turn for the unusual! Elijah ordered that four water pots full of water be brought to the altar's side. Quickly a shuffling stir rippled through the crowded onlookers as several people ran to comply with the prophets words. Soon, one by one, the large pots were brought alongside the stately standing altar. Elijah now gave a most different instruction, "Pour all of the water from all four pots on the offering and the wood that is to be burned!" At this command, a sound of surprise escaped the puzzled crowd! This would only make the offering unlikely to burn! What was the prophet doing? He seemed to be insuring the failure of his sacrifice by this odd action.

As if the first pouring of water weren't enough, Elijah issued the same order a second time! And again several men in the crowd disappeared through the mass of people only to reappear sometime later with overflowing water pots. And again the water was poured out over the bull offering, the wood and the down over the entire altar.

Now, all of us who were watching were stunned to silence. There could be no human fire that would ignite such a drenched, watery offering. Elijah the prophet was not finished. He again gave the same order and again four large water pots were fetched and emptied over the already soggy, dripping, water logged altar. So much water had been pour over the altar that the trench had filled with its reddish water mixture and overflowed onto the ground surrounding the area.

Now, Elijah waited. The prophets of Baal, in their bloodied exhausted condition could only watch now with all of the rest of Israel. The prophet waited! The prophets of

Baal waited! The people waited! The king, who had watched in rapt fascination also waited. As the sky changed and the hour moved toward the time of appointed evening sacrifice, Elijah slowly walked to the altar. It still dripped with water and blood and the ground around it was still stained with blood and water and now mud and small puddles dotted the ground around the base of the 12 stones. All eyes were on Elijah! As he stood near the altar he lifted his head ever so slight to heaven and said, "Yahweh, God of Abraham, Isaac, and Israel, today let it be known that You are God in Israel and I am Your servant, and that at Your word, I have done all these things. Answer me, LORD! Answer me so that this people will know that You, Yahweh, are God and that You have turned their hearts back."

The silence over the area was deafening! No one moved, no one spoke, I am not sure anyone could even breathe with the sense of awe and consecration that infused the mood.

The sky over head was clear and empty of cloud and wind. With the 3 years of drought and famine still upon us, the clearness of the sky and its emptiness had become a daily curse to us. We had grown accustomed to its glaring, merciless heat and complete lack of moisture; today had been no different.

Suddenly, without warning and without explanation, a long blazing shaft of fire spiked to the earth from the sky immediately above the altar. It cracked and hissed like a flash of lightening, but it began out of nowhere and angled toward Elijah's altar. This bolt of scorching flame touched down on the offering, wood, altar and water, traveling the full length of the stones height and consumed all that was in its way. Bull, wood, stone, dust were instantly melted with fervent heat and reduced to nothing but scattered ashes, the mud and the excess water being licked up by the thirsty flashing inferno. In the few brief moments it took the pillar of fire to fall and reduce the sacrifice to nothing, the people panicked, screamed in utter fear and fell to their faces. Their only words were, "Yahweh, He is God! Yahweh, He is God!"

With this smell of smoke and flame still in the air, Elijah turned his attention to his competition. The prophets of Baal were now beginning to disband and trail off into the country side to hide having been soundly humiliated, but Elijah was not done. Quickly he commanded over the noise of the dispersing crowds of people, "Seize the prophets of Baal! Do not let even one of them escape."

The people, still reeling from the demonstration of God's power, responded immediately and rounded up every prophet within reach and according to orders marched them off toward the Kishon valley wadi. Soon Elijah joined them there where a great slaughter ensued.

I had stood quietly with King Ahab who had not spoken a word nor moved any great distance, except for some nervous pacing and shuffling, while the punishment was carried out. Although he did not say so, I am sure there were moments when he feared for his life at the return of the prophet. As the judgment upon the false prophets was being completed in the distance Elijah returned to the King at the base of Mount Carmel and rather than vengeance, he had something else on his mind. To my utter surprise, he announced to Ahab that he was to prepare himself a celebration meal in honor of the end of the famine, "Go up, eat and drink, for there is the sound of a rainstorm" he declared to Ahab as he passed him and began a slow deliberate ascent to the mountain's top.

With those words firmly in hand and the view of the prophet Elijah climbing the steep side of the mount to its summit, Ahab and I began organizing the servants, gathering the royal trappings and gear and thus, simply making every effort for the quickest journey possible back to Jezreel. We worked as fast as we could, given the limited number of people available to help and every chance I got, I stopped to watch, in the distance, the prophet and his servant as they stood looking out over the Great Sea from the top of Mt. Carmel. Sometimes it looked as though the two were standing together looking, at other times it looked as if Elijah was crouching or kneeling while his servant stood looking out over the water. This pattern continued for several minutes, together then apart, together and then apart, the prophet crouching and his servant going to look out over the water.

Watching and working to get ready to travel, gave me only scattered glimpses of the top of the mountain, but when I did have a good look, it seemed that nothing else was being done on the summit but kneeling and watching. Was the prophet digging again in the dirt? Was he picking up objects on the ground? Was the servant watching for something in particular? What was this curious pattern of crouching and watching to mean? Did it have anything to do with the sound of a rainstorm that Elijah had mentioned? Somehow I knew it did, I just didn't know how at this point.

We were finally ready to go with the last step being to mount our horses; this included readying the King's chariot by securing its poles and the horse's straps. With that done, all that was left was to climb in and hold on. As the bridles, shoulder and belly straps on the horses were being tightened, a voice came calling to me from toward the mountain. It was the Prophet Elijah's servant. He was running as fast as he could and bringing urgent news! The prophet had sent him to urge us quickly on to Jezreel BEFORE the storm overtook us.

Rain! Storm! Was this the sound that Elijah had heard and was it now fast approaching? It didn't take long before the sky over the mountain as far north and south as I could see began to darken and the wind, which had previously been nonexistent, was beginning to blow. At first a few drops of rain began lightly falling across our preparation area and then accompanied by stronger wind and a low roaring sound. A wall of torrential downpour began moving in over the mountain and down the slope toward us. Immediately King Ahab climbed into his chariot and with a maddening dash, the entire royal party moved off the hill side and down into the valley below, trying with every ounce of our strength to out run the rain. Down through the Kishon valley to the east we sped along toward the capitol city and the palace.

That day had begun with the entire nation gathering

to witness the power of Jehovah, proving Himself superior to the feeble powerless antics of the god Baal. It had continued with the prophets of Baal being humiliated and destroyed and at the close of the day, the people of Israel had reinstituted their loyalty to the Lord God. It indeed, had been a day of Historical proportions after all. And now the day was coming to a close with a spreading storm of rain reaching out across the land. After three years without rain, just the smell of fresh moisture was intoxicating to us all. And as the rain pelted our faces while we drove hard through the storm I thought to myself, "What more could be added to such a glorious day?", then, just off to my left and over, next to the King's chariot, I saw a running, sprinting, galloping human figure moving past all of us.

Who was this super human being outrunning us all in a driving rain storm? For a fleeting second I could make no sense of what I was seeing, but as he dashed past me, I then knew. In that moment I recognized the prophet. It was Elijah, the prophet of God, with his mantle tucked under his belt and a slight smile on his chiseled face. And being held buoyant by the power of God, he was in a full velocity run for Jezreel and he would, no doubt, be there before us all!

CHAPTER TEN:
JESUS AND THE SEA OF GALILEE
MATTHEW 14 AND MARK 4

Historical background and setting

The year was approximately 26-30 A.D. Jesus of Nazareth was in full time ministry in and around the Sea of Galilee with his crew of disciples, apostles and other followers. Later he would journey to Jerusalem, where he would eventually be crucified, never to return to this pristine area of northern Israel. The Sea of Galilee, also called Lake of Gennesaret, or Lake Tiberius, is the largest **freshwater lake** in **Israel**, at approximately 33 miles in circumference, about 13 miles long, and 8 miles wide. The lake has a maximum depth of approximately 141 feet and lies just over 700 ft **below sea level** making it the lowest freshwater lake on Earth and a unique geographical area for much of the gospel narrative to be recorded.

The Story

Jesus of Nazareth had many followers and many who called themselves his disciples. Among the closest to him were those we called 'the twelve'; after that a much larger group which he also called and sent out who were about seventy strong. It was to this group that I belonged; an anonymous, unnamed follower who came to believe strongly in his Messianic message. It was with a number of this group of seventy that I traveled in and around the Galilee area with the teacher and his chosen twelve apostles. Though unnamed, I was none the less present to watch and join the journey of those days. This is my story.

The Sea of Galilee is a rich fishery. The largest lake in all of Palestine produces tons of fish caught by hundreds of fisherman throughout all seasons. These catches supply a substantial amount of food for the Hebrew people who live on and around the sea, not to mention supplies of fish that are taken, as they are available, to the larger cities. Galilee, which is fed by numerous deep underground springs and of course, the legendary Jordan River, figures greatly in the way of life for all Hebrews of northern Israel. I have been a fisherman all of my life, as my father had been before me and his father before him. I have lived on the water and made my living by knowing the Sea and its ways. Not knowing the sea and its habits could cost a man dearly in his business ventures and his own physical well being as the waters and wind of the Galilee can be dangerous, indeed. I pride myself in being able to respect the sea, and at the same time, work with it to provide a living for me and my family. It was not until the teacher from Nazareth arrived on the scene that I learned some astounding lessons about faith and trust and who ultimately held sway over the wind and sea.

I had heard the summons of the teacher when he came to our lake shores calling upon all to follow him. He promised to make us *fishers of me*, if we did follow, and this strange idea of becoming *fishers of men* intrigued me greatly. I had been a fisher of fish with great success, but did not know what fishing for men was all about. That is until listening to the words of this Jesus who came from Nazareth and who many said came from God. As I had watched him and listened to his instructions, I had determined to follow him and find out how he would in fact fish for men.

Joining with the twelve as part of the other seventy disciples meant that we often spent days on end with Jesus, trying to capture the meaning of his teaching and watching the incredible displays of power that accompanied his travels and speaking. These displays of power served to convince many, including myself, that this one could be God's chosen Messiah sent to Israel. Jesus and the twelve apostles, along with many of the numbered seventy, crisscrossed the whole of the nation for several years before those fateful days of his crucifixion and resurrection. I was honored to have been able to accompany them on many of those excursions. In particular, many excursions they made in and around the great inland Sea of Galilee. Some call it the Sea of Tiberius, others call it the Lake of Gennesaret, but all who work there and sail her waters call her fickle and treacherous at times, due to the sudden storms and wind that can spring up and badger those who fish her depths and sail her changing surface. It was in several of these kinds of situations that I saw the Messiah's power first hand and came to believe in him and his message. Let me tell you about two such episodes that stand out directly in my mind.

One such occasion was truly remarkable and not only involved the Savior and the sea, but one of the most outspoken of his apostles as well. We had been involved for a very long trying day with a large crowd of people who had followed Jesus into the countryside to hear him preach. As the day wore on and it became obvious that these people were prepared to stay until dusk, Jesus had decided that all of them needed to be fed. Through a truly unbelievable feeding process, Jesus had taken one boy's small lunch and had miraculously fed well over 5,000 people. It had been all of us, his disciples, who had organized the huge crowd and distributed the bread and fish to every man, woman and child who sat near the shore of Galilee and listened to the teacher's word.

As the day closed and the last of the food had been given away, Jesus very specifically instructed us to get into the boat and proceed across the lake ahead of him. Our fishing boat lay moored just on the edge of the water, waiting for us to shove off from the sand and rock, make for deeper water and trim the sail. At the time we thought nothing of the request for us to leave him behind, because we were accustomed to such actions. Looking back now, it was as if Jesus was sending us into a very deliberate test of faith, a test that would illustrate so clearly his sovereign power. So it was with the persuasion of Jesus that we made our way onto the fishing vessel, while Jesus stayed to mingle with the dispersing throng, encouraging them as they left and to direct them on their way home. We, on the other hand, were heading out across the main expanse of the lake to the south eastern shore in the general area of the cities of Gadara and Gergesa. It was somewhat unusual to leave the teacher behind when much more ministry was already planned, but then at times, as was his habit, he would withdraw from the crowds and from us and spend many hours in prayer. It was this that we assumed he intended to do, since such a glorious, but exhausting time was spent with the masses early in the day.

As the boat was maneuvered into deeper water with pole and oar and the main sail lifted to catch the wind, we started our way into the evening. Immediately, it became clear that our journey would not be an easy one. The wind was contrary to our desired direction and was periodically buffeting us from either side, so as to make progress difficult and slow. Being forced to row and tact into the wind, great white foamed wave breakers sprayed over the bow. As each wave crashed, we were caught in the water as it spread over and down upon us. The rolling surf would lift us at a slight angle upward and then let us drop with a hard smack back against the sea beneath us. The repeated cycles of splashing waves and pounding back to the water's surface set us all on edge as we feverishly worked at keeping the boat on course. We were not concerned with capsizing, in this particular incident, but were more concerned with our physical strength waning and the ship being pushed by the wind in unwanted directions. Thus, we struggled against the wind to move forward. There was no time really, to think of what Jesus may or may not be doing, we had left him on land to pray alone, expecting somehow that he would meet us at our destination or catch up with us. And now we were engaged in a battle with the forces of Lake Galilee. The tug of war between the wind and our vastly inferior muscle power continued well into the night and early morning.

About 3 o'clock in the morning, one of the disciples sitting bravely toward the bow of the vessel called to us to look out off the leeward side of the boat. He had noticed something strange out on the water some distance from us. With his urgent call, each of us stained to look over the seas surface into the wind. With difficulty we attempted to stare through the misty spray that still fanned out over us from time to time as the boat slapped again and again against the water.

What we saw was strange indeed. Gliding over the water's surface, buffeted gently by the wind, was a gray white shimmering figure of a man! As the realization of what we were seeing came slowly to us like a lengthening shadow under the evening sun, we grew trepid and fearful. This could not be a man! No such man could walk the surface of the water and certainly not in this kind of wind. Were we seeing a ghost or spirit drifting over the waves? Why was it coming our way? What could we have done to warrant such an aberration? As the figure closed the distance between us our fear only escalated with each closing step. At this point, several cried out into the night sky, speaking to no one in particular, but rather to just expend the buildup of terror and emotion that raced though all of our minds and hearts.

With these sudden outbursts of trauma being blurted into the air from all who sat stunned in the boat, a distant call of comfort came traveling back to us. Over the water in the spray and mist came the words, "Have courage! It is I! Do not be afraid!" These words carried the all too familiar ring of the Savior's voice! What we saw approaching us on the water and what we were hearing in our ears did not seem to match and yet there in front of us all, Jesus was coming to us, literally walking on the water. He was in full stride, as if walking down any of a thousand dusty Judean roads, each step that he took bearing the full force of his weight, but showing no sign of dipping beneath the water's surface. Waves rolled under him, lifting him and then letting him down with the greatest of ease. White caps billowed up and broke around him, but did little to stop his movements. In his hair were the signs of a stiffly blowing wind and his robe bristled and flapped with the winds movements, but it had no ill effect on his balance or his progress. What began as a distant grey white shadowy figure, now stood out to us against the dark blue black background of the sea and the early morning sky. We could now see clearly the comforting sight of the Lord's whitish robe and blue shoulder wrapped sash, along with his soothing smile and glinting eyes and thus, we were immediately calmed and quieted.

The relief of this discovery had but a few moments to settle over us, when booming over our heads came a strong and distinctive voice. It was Peter, one the twelve and one of the Teacher's most loyal followers. "Lord," he yelled into the wind, "If that is you, command me to come to you on the water." With the drama of the earlier experience just finished; now all heads were turned toward the apostle and the drama was instantly renewed! What could he be thinking? The wind and waves were still roaring around us and the last thing on any one's mind was getting out of the boat! And it was one thing for the Lord's Messiah to walk on the water, but one of us? This did not fit into my framework of discipleship training and possibilities. The bulk of the disciple crew were sitting or lying low in the framework of the boat's seating and fishing capacity. Most, if not holding to oars or poles, were grasping on to equipment or rigging or leaning hard against the inside of the ship's side railing. This particular vessel was designed with low sides and a steep stern and bow. This would accommodate strong men needing to lean out over the water to pull in nets full of wiggling, writhing fish, but in the full force of such strong winds, we were all forced to sit low or crouch against some support to remain out of harm's way.

It was from this awkward position, with all of us low and hiding from the wind, that a strong compelling voice returned to us though the whistling wind. In almost one unified twisting of the head, we were looking in the direction of the voice and heard the Teacher call Peter toward the water. With our amazed eyes trained on this leader among us, he moved cautiously to the ship's edge and stood leaning against the wind. He pulled his robe up to well above his knees, tucking and tying it under his belt. Then, sitting uncomfortably on the rounded top of the ship's side rail, slipped out of his sandals, lifted first one leg, then the other and slowly pivoted out over the water. With the wind and waves rocking the boat from side to side, the water's surface would rhythmically swell upward along the ship's side, as if to offer quick access to the icy deep; if someone so desired.

Waiting and timing his first step, he watched the lake rise to meet him and, as the foaming twisting liquid greeted him, he stepped onto the water! I was certain that this impetuous disciple would end up being sucked under the lake's surface, soaked to the bone and then fished out again by the rest of us. BUT NOT SO! As this large framed man leaned into the water, it held him! As his next step pressed the water's top edge, it held as well. Soon Peter was taking step after step out along the top of the frothing mass which moved under him, all the while gazing toward the Lord with wide eyes and nervous hand and arm motions. Being pummeled and clawed by the wind and lashed several times by cutting stinging bursts of water did not seem to initially faze the apostle. His faith and energy kept pushing him across the struggling sea. Although none of us did so, I felt as if we could have leapt to our feet and cheered this daring feat. But, of course, we were still holding on for dear life to the ship ourselves, so such boisterous expression would have been dangerous for us.

Those of us fearful souls, who remained immovable in the ship, really could not believe our eyes! Here we were bobbing feverishly in a crude fishing boat, with the Sea of Galilee swirling fiercely around us and the Messiah and Peter were gliding toward one another as they skimmed the surface of the watery lake. IT WAS UNBELIEVEABLE! And yet, we were watching it happen right in front of us.

The eerie awe of the moment came to a sudden pause when Peter's voice was heard in the wind with strong tinges of distress! "Lord, save me!" he cried out to the Jesus. The apostle, who was famous for his sudden reactions and quick responses, was now haltering and losing focus. The wind, driving against the bearded face of the apostle, with its constant grabbing and tugging at Peter's robe, pulled his eyes from the Savior. The sharp, cold discomfort of spraying sea water added to the distraction of the man as he struggled forward. He had cried for help because he was beginning to sink into a black deep watery brush with death. All of us, still awe struck by the scene before us, now held our breath as we were sure this daring disciple would perish in the rolling waves.

Immediately, however, Jesus was within reach of Peter. In an instant, he had closed the distance between them and caught Peter by the arm. As the two of them embraced, Peter was pulled immediately to the surface, braced by the support of the Savior's own strength. Then, in a few short steps, both of them glided the rest of the distance to the ship and reached to grip the railing at the edge of the decking. As they pressed to the side of the ship and prepared a quick climb into its safe confines, the storm suddenly dissolved into nothing. The wind's rage, in a moment of time, became a whimper and then a whisper. The waves, once fierce and looming, now settled to a serene calm. Who was this man? What was this power he possessed? We could not find adequate words to even speak at such a moment. He, on the other hand, quietly and reassuringly spoke to Peter as they finished their climb into the boat, "You of little faith, why did you doubt?" he said.

As the last small waves flattened under us and the boat, as well as the sea, became placid and smooth, we who had been spell bound with fright and excitement by what had transpired just minutes before, now could do nothing but worship! Some on their faces, others on their knees, a few weeping gently and whispering to themselves, all could only confess that truly this was the Son of God! And of course, there was none more worshipful AND grateful than Peter himself!

On a second occasion involving Jesus and the sea, we had a similar experience, but this time no one got out of the boat; indeed the miracle AND lesson of faith happen with all of us in it! Again, Jesus, his disciples and a large crowd of people were assembled for teaching. We were on the western shore of the great lake and the crowd had grown and grown over the afternoon hours. In a wide area between the shoreline and the main road north and south, a few miles south of the City Capernaum, the teaching was to begin. After those of us who were with him tried to organize the patrons and curiosity seekers for the Lord's instruction, with little success, Jesus decided that the best approach was to preach from the boat! So, with Jesus sitting in the fishing vessel and the crowd gathered on the shore, the afternoon of parables and stories and pointed instruction took place.

As evening was beginning to approach and the teaching sessions came to a close for the day, Jesus, still sitting quietly on the shore-side of the boat, instructed us to cross over to the other side of the lake. People were slowly dispersing and orienting themselves to their journey home for the night while we scrambled to make ready the ship for open water. Several disciples pushed hard at the long poles to edge the boat away from the shallows, while others prepared to hoist the sail up along the mast and turn the boom with the wind. Disciples spread out over the deck and found their places to disperse the weight evenly across the entire length and width of the vessel. With everything in place, the weight of the ship bow slowly cut through the water's surface toward the deeper lake.

On this sailing exploration we were not alone. Looking up from my place near the stern of the ship, I glanced starboard, forward and then to the port side over the lake's horizon and was taken aback by the scene! Apparently not all of the people had disbursed from the shoreline to head for home. Scattered around us, numerous sailing vessels bobbed and dipped with the lake's cadence. These curious sailors formed a flotilla of sorts to accompany us over to the other side, probably with the intent of catching another installment of the Messiah's teaching. I was amazed at the insistence and dedication many were showing in making the effort to stay close to the Chosen One. So, as evening lengthened an armada of fishing boats sailed together across the Sea of Galilee with, the now sleeping, Jesus in the center boat and the center of attention.

For the first hour or so we plowed water and cut through the increasing waves with a normal pattern of gentle rises and gentle falls, joining the tempo of the other boats in a concert of sailing maneuvers and movement. Then, as we seemed to approach our midway mark, the wind suddenly swept in and around us, whipping and churning the once cooperative lake water into an enemy of spray, waves and fierce splashing. Taking stock of the situation soon told us that every other sailing entity within view was experiencing the same thing. Mainsails of all sizes and shapes were being trimmed or lowered all across the lake in a unified effort to gain as much control as was possible over the ship's tillers and rudders and still make forward progress. Although a few of the smaller vessels were forced to turned back, most of the remaining boats then simply continued on, trying desperately to out run the storm.

Under normal conditions, a strong wind could be harnessed enough to get the vessel to shore quickly so the storm could be waited out. On this occasion, however, the fierce wind was raising giant waves and sending them up and over the side of the ship in such frequency that we were being swamped. Crashing wave after wave was bringing pounding layers of water over us and into the boat, filling up our living space faster than anyone could bail or carry it back to its place. If this kept up for very long, the entire ship would fill with water, capsize and plunge to the depths.

In the confusion that surfaced in our boat over the wind and filling waves, everyone had ignored Jesus, who was sleeping on a small cushion in the stern of the ship, not too far from where I sat. There, undisturbed, unruffled and seeming unaware of the storm, slept Jesus. While we struggled against what looked like an inevitable capsizing and fought back at the wind's attack, Jesus had remained sleeping and restful, not showing the slightest twitch or shudder in reaction to the storm.

This was not the case for us! Panic had spread through every heart and the face of every disciple was one of fear and dread. Finally, the stricken leaders of our expedition could wait no longer and rushed to awaken the sleeping son of God, "Teacher! Teacher!" they yelled through the deafening wind. "Don't you care that we are going to die out here?" they continued as one made a quick effort to shake the teachers shoulder.

Opening his eyes suddenly and taking in the panic and turbulence that surrounded him, he sat up from his cushion. Then, he purposely rose to one knee, braced himself against one of the disciple's back, raised the rest of his full height and turned to face the wind. I am not sure what the crew expected of him at his point, but whatever it was it did not include what he actually did at that moment. Facing full into the wind, with furrowed brow and focused eyes, he spoke directly to the storm itself. "Silence, be still!" he declared, giving the wind a stern rebuke! His words had no more left his mouth and pierced the driving air, when the wind began to drop and die, decreasing to a dead calm. The ship gave several final pitches and then became still. Faint sounds of distant voices carried briefly to our ears from the other vessels as they reacted to the calming wind and water. I stood in shock at the silence and calm around me, noticing only the gentle tickle of water drops making their slow ride down my face and cheeks and dropping to the wet wood under my sandals. Slowly my racing heart joined the serenity and peace that now prevailed around us all!

The silence that prevailed for several minutes was only interrupted by Jesus himself. Firmly, but lovingly he simply said to us all, "Why are you so fearful? Do you still have no faith?" Our terror toward the storm now turned to terror of another kind. We were terrified at what we had just seen and the power we had just experienced. As Jesus turned to find his cushion again, we who were still stunned by this display of authority, as well as our own obvious lack of faith, could only turn to those closest to us and ponder this man's true identity. "Who was he...really? Even the waves and the sea obey him!"

This Jesus of Nazareth had taken his well meaning, but immature disciples and apostles, sent them out on a lake that they all thought they were familiar with and created two spectacular life lessons that unveiled their frail humanity against a glorious backdrop of his perfect love and sovereignty. I don't think we or the Sea of Galilee will ever be the same!

CHAPTER ELEVEN:
NEBUCHADNEZZAR'S FURNACE
DANIEL 3

Historical background and setting

The year was approximately 605-597 B.C. The Babylonian empire led by King Nebuchadnezzar II has invaded and conquered Israel. In a few short years he would return to Jerusalem and destroy the city. In the meantime he has taken thousands of Israelites from the royal family line and the nobility and brought them captive into exile to the city of Babylon. Among these captives is one Daniel and his three Hebrew companions, who are given Babylonian names; Shadrach, Meshach and Abednego. These are taken to the King's palace and groomed for special service to the King. As the pages of the Old Testament book of Daniel open, we see Daniel and the three companions finding favor with Nebuchadnezzar, due to Daniel's interpretation of the King's dream. As a reward, these four Hebrew's are given positions of authority to govern in the land of Babylon. It is from these positions of rule that Daniel's three friends will have a dramatic confrontation with the King of Babylon.

The Story

I am a Babylonian prefect, appointed by the King's palace to govern a small province of Babylon and thus found myself among the many satraps, governors, advisers, treasurers, judges, magistrates, and all the others rulers of the provinces that were invited, or should I say required, to attend a special dedication. I am nameless in the biblical narrative, never the less, I am present among the great throng of people that witness this great event and, in the process, witness a colossal miracle given by the God of the Hebrews to King Nebuchadnezzar and the Babylonian people. This is my story.

The nation was abuzz with talk that our King Nebuchadnezzar had been secretly building an enormous image for the Babylonian people. In the plain of Dura, located just south of the City of Babylon proper, he had been preparing his image and waiting for the right time to have it dedicated. At long last the image was ready and all of the leaders of Babylon from across the entire empire were invited to attend his grand dedication of the image. Although we were given an official invitation, it was commonly understood that failing to attend could mean loss of our position in the government, possible imprisonment or even death. So we came with our families and servants by the thousands to gather and behold this great building project in all of its glory.

Arriving at the capitol, I had no real concept of what to expect. Had we come to see an image of one of the great Babylonian gods? Marduk? Tammuz? Nabu? The Babylonian pantheon of gods was numerous and each, I suppose, worthy of a new image. So I came with curiosity, as well as suspicion, knowing that our King could be known to surprise us all with his plans. Coming through the city and exiting the southern gate toward the area of Dura, a flat and exposed area of land with wide visibility brought a surge of excitement, as I could see in the distance a tall dark vague image towering over the valley where it stood. Thousands of others were making their way closer to the image, many jostling to get in position for the best view of the image and the celebration that would soon begin. I, like most everyone else, was swept up in the momentum of the masses as they slowly crawled in close to the center of activity around this huge figure in the distance.

While children ran and played, families and dignitaries made their way through the press to the best positions available. Conversations were developing everywhere while people mingled and watched and generally waited while additional hundreds came ever closer to the image. Having already seen the image at some distance, I made it my direct focus as I led my family closer and closer to its prominent stance near the King's royal tent and platform. As I moved closer, the finer detail of the image began to come into view. It was not a familiar sight that I beheld. No deity of Chaldean origin came immediately to mind, in fact the image seemed to resemble a man; a human; a giant massive form that was more human than god-like. Although there was no official description or title giving the image an identity, the image had a vague Kingly form, as if to capture in one iconic representation, all of the noble Chaldean leaders over the centuries, including our fearless King Nebuchadnezzar!

The colossal statue stood 90 feet tall from its broad base to the top of it intricately carved head. This put the full height of the figure at twice the elevation of Babylon's great wall and magnificent main gate! I marveled at the image and its workmanship. In its full gold composition and 9 foot width, it stood sentinel over the whole Dura plain and indeed, as I am sure it was intended, over the whole of the Kingdom. I watched as leaders from across the provinces would approach this mysterious figure, still squinting in the sun and bantering with friends, then slowly shuffling to a stop. Then they would look the full length up the gold surface of this creature and stand with mouths gapping and words failing them. The King's image was capturing the wonder of a nation!

I had only met the three Hebrew governors briefly prior to this occasion and though I knew they would be faithful to attend the dedication, I wondered what they were thinking as I watched them approach the image. No doubt this whole affair could be problematic for them, as I knew they adhered to very strict religious guidelines in their worship of their Hebrew god. They stood like all of the rest of us gazing in stunned reaction to the view before them, but as they moved to within an arm's length of me, I could tell that their assessment of this giant object of worship was much less subdued. These three stood silent and somber amidst the clamor that surrounded them.

Soon the King and the royal party could be seen at the side of the massive base of the figure along with a small cadre of officials who appeared to be readying a proclamation of some kind to the gathered people. One prominent man finally stepped forward to the front of a long platform and signaled for our attention. Slowly the immense gathering quieted itself to the sound of the single voice projecting from the front. "Welcome leaders and people of Babylon!" he began, "Please observe that when you hear the sound of the vast array of instruments, you are to fall down and worship the statute that our great King Nebuchadnezzar has set up!" At this word, a twitter of nervous excitement and reaction rippled through the crowd. As good Chaldeans, we were accustomed to honoring deities of every kind and nature.

It had always seemed to us that the world around us was a complicated place and no doubt governed by many supernatural forces and divine entities, so to be introduced to another with such a spectacular visual image seemed an honor. Glancing at my Hebrew counterparts however, proved that they did not share our pleasure. Their faces were grim and disturbed! The herald continued with the King's command, "If however, you do not fall down and worship at the sound of the music, you will be immediately thrown into a furnace of blazing fire!" This was a sudden inclusion of instruction that took many of us by surprise! We were surprised, not so much at the threat of punishment, as this was a common expectation, but rather at the severity of the punishment. Death by burning in a furnace seemed extreme even for us.

Immediately sensing the tension in the air increase and hearing the low and slow gasps of the people around me, I turned slightly to observe what might be the reaction of the three Hebrews; Shadrach, Meshach and Abednego. Their faces showed me little except their resolve. From the meaning of the firmness in their facial features, my mind immediately drew a horrible conclusion. These Hebrews could not comply. In fact, I should say *would not* comply! The mingled scores of people directly around us paid little attention to what I saw on their faces. Everyone was only focused on their own responsibility to bow and worship so as to save their own lives and I would not blame any of them, since this was foremost on my mind as well.

Soon my thinking was drawn back to the front of the great gathering as the bold sound of horn, flute, zither, lyre, harp, and every kind of music imaginable danced out across the heads of the nervous crowd. As the sound reached the people and spread like a gentle breeze over us, nothing was now heard but the sound of shuffling feet, rustling cloth and garments, the scraping of dirt and rocks and whispers, groans and sighs. From the front to the back, with staggered tempo, the entire mass of people began dropping to their knees and faces to pay homage to the great likeness before them. I was not about to risk my life or that of my family, so I quickly slipped to the ground and bowed my head to the soil below, motioning to my wife and children to do the same. It was in this shift to the ground that I saw again, in the direction of the Hebrew men, their staunch resolve. Twisting my head to the side from its place in the dust to view these three defiant people brought into view a frightening scene. There was no bowing or worship; no compliance or submission; only sandaled feet, trousered legs, hemmed robes and dangling sashes with a few miscellaneous personal items on the ground around them. Each of these defiant men remained erect and bold in their original places!

This act of defiance in itself could have been missed by those in the front near the statue, who were concerned that the proclamation be strictly enforced. Since these Hebrew were some distance from them, however, several of my countrymen who had witnessed their failure to bow took strong exception to this rebellious act and let old wounds open their hearts to malicious motive. In their minds, this was a perfect opportunity to seek revenge and retribution for some unnamed, undefined offence. So, with a quick and ready evil report, a small group of people from where we were positioned ventured to the front and conferred with the officials in charge.

As I watched from my place at the side of the three, it was obvious that the report had caused an instant stir around the royal tent. Rapid movement with urgent voices could be seen and heard, along with what looked like the King himself making a flurry of sudden moves to make his way through the crowd and proceed to our location. Out ahead of us the mass of people began parting and dividing, as if slowly sliced with a sharp blade and in the vortex of the cutting, came King Nebuchadnezzar himself. After making his way a short distance into the throng of people, he stopped in a furious rage and commanded that the three Hebrew leaders be brought to the front. With instantaneous obedience, several guards rushed the rest of the way through the crowd to the Hebrews and securely apprehended each one and ushered them to the front for all of us to see.

With this sudden turn of events, the great mass of humanity that stood watching began a new round of nervous chatter and whispering. What would become of these men? Would the King follow through with his threat? Was their offence really worthy of such punishment? It would only be a matter of a few minutes before all of us would see the results of both the King's fury AND the protection of the God of Israel over his chosen ones. And for those results, I made my way closer to the great tall figure so that I would not miss what was about to transpire.

At the sound of the King's voice, the huge gathering again fell silent. "It is true, Shadrach, Meshach and Abednego, that you don't serve my gods or worship the golden image that I have set up?" the King snorted at the Hebrews. Continuing, he issued a final challenge, "Now if you are ready, I will once again start the music so that you can fall down and worship the statue; but if you do not, you will be immediately thrown into the furnace - and who is the god who can rescue you from my power?"

The three Hebrews hesitated not one moment in their reply. "Nebuchadnezzar, we don't need to give you an answer to this question. If the God we serve exists, then He can rescue us from the furnace of blazing fire and He can rescue us from your power, Oh King!" At these words, the people who were close enough to hear them bristled in reaction. These were daring words indeed to speak to the King. Shadrach, Meshach and Abednego continued, "But, even if He does not rescue us, you must know that we will not serve your gods or worship the gold statue you set up." The shock at such insubordination was instant as it stretched out to grip the entire assembly. These three were signing their own death certificates and personally volunteering for the furnace!

The King was furious with rage and wrath, his strain and stress was so severe that his countenance was altered and his face misshapen grotesquely as he fumed and paced before the crowd and the three Hebrew men. After several moments had passed, the orders came bellowing out over the crowd. The furnace was to be increased in its heat seven times hotter than normal and several of his strongest solders available were to tie the three defiant ones hand and foot and throw them into the burning furnace. The Hebrew men were dressed in their customary trousers, robes, head coverings and other clothes that distinguished them as men of Hebrew decent AND Babylonian in their authoritative positions of governing. They were bound hand and foot; clothes and all; and carried to the great mouth of the furnace.

The imposing brick furnace was flickering shades of red, orange and yellow over its entire surface as it was stoked over and over and over again to bring the temperature up to the commanded level. As the temperature increased, the people moved further and further away from the brazen chamber of fire. Heat waves rippled and quivered in the air as the furnace and the surrounding stone, rock and soil became devastatingly hot. It seemed that at the center of the furnaces box was molten fire billowing and churning inside, almost ready to consume the furnace itself. With this raging heat, each of the three Hebrews was carried by the appointed soldiers to the front of the furnace and thrown, tumbling and twisting onto the floor of the furnace. As they each hit and rolled in the super charged coals and flames, brilliant bursts of glowing sparks exploded and shot in every direction. The soldiers who had been given the morbid job of carrying the Hebrews could not stand the intense heat. As their hands released the men into the fire, they themselves burst into flame! Their clothes, their hair, their skin, even their armor instantly flickered with flames and combustion. The inferno killed them on the spot and the whole of the gathering watched in horror as their bodies rolled smoking and bubbling with shoots and flashes of flame. There was no doubt that the Hebrews would be consumed in but a moment.

The anguish and disgust in the crowd was palatable, but short lived! Suddenly the King was up jumping and shouting frantically to his advisors, "Didn't we throw three men, bound, into the fire?" he screamed. "Look, I see four men, not even tied but walking around in the fire unharmed; and the fourth looks like a son of the gods." The advisors confirmed they had thrown but three into the fire, but now as they all gathered at the mouth of the furnace and gazed through the shimmering heat into the billowing flames on the inside, there indeed were four men. All four were standing in the flames, untied and unharmed. The fire still raged all around them with crackling and popping noises, dancing flames flashed everywhere, the heat waves still billowed and wiggled in mid air around the furnace, but these four walked unharmed in it all. It looked as though they were talking amongst themselves and listening intently at the words of this mysterious and baffling fourth man.

King Nebuchadnezzar and his advisors at first stood stunned and shocked at what they were watching! Eventually the King, straining his neck and head from side to side and bending and squinting his way toward the door of the furnace, called through the heat to Shadrach, Meshach, and Abednego. "You servants of the Most High God—come out!' the King called as the four walked casually among the blistering coals of the furnace. The three Hebrew men stepped away from the licking flames and through the furnace's opening one at a time, first Shadrach, then Meshach and then Abednego. The King, along with his advisors and the gasping crowd of people behind them, watched in amazement. From my vantage point I could see them clearly and it appeared that they were completely unharmed. Nothing burned, charred or singed could be seen. As the three gathered in front of the staring royal leaders, many of the satraps, prefects and governors pressed in close to see for themselves. Touching and poking at them, their clothes were examined, their skin and hair inspected, everything about them was scrutinized and yet nothing was found to be out of order. I watched as several men from the King's court even leaned close to the three attempting to catch the smell of smoke on their clothing and yet, none could be detected. Energy and excitement now flashed through the whole assembly one more time as the realization of what had just happened settled over them. Now, the people could hardly restrain themselves from pressing in as close as possible hoping to touch these miracle survivors.

The King, now shaken by the dramatic rescue performed by the Hebrew god, began motioning to all of his advisors, gathering them together around him. Then with a sudden and deliberate show of determination, he stepped to the front of the great gathering and projected his voice strongly out over our heads with a hastily formulated proclamation, "Praise to the God of Shadrach, Meshach, and Abednego! He sent His angel and rescued His servants who trusted in Him. They violated my command and risked their lives rather than worship any god except their own God. Therefore I issue a decree that anyone of any people, nation, or language who says anything offensive against the God of Shadrach, Meshach, and Abednego will be torn limb from limb and his house made a garbage dump. There is no other god who is able to deliver like this."

I stood alone for several minutes attempting to sort through my emotions and thoughts. Just hours ago I had joined my leadership companions for what was to be a formal introduction by our King of a new Chaldean deity. With great pomp and fanfare, he had revealed his great image and called us all to bow our knee to it. We had all expected a unanimous response of allegiance from all who had gathered only to see three Hebrew men choose to risk death rather than comply with the King's command.

This, however, was not the most significant development of the day! Fully expecting to watch Shadrach, Meshach and Abednego burn to death in a fiery furnace that was hot enough to instantly kill all who even came near it, we saw nothing of the sort. Rather, we witnessed the God of Israel whom these three Hebrews worshipped and served fervently, stand with them in the furnace flames preserving them entirely. Never had we seen such divine power and demonstration from our Chaldean menagerie of gods; our King Nebuchadnezzar knew it as he gazed into the burning inferno he had created.

This Jehovah of the Hebrews had proven to all of us that he deserved the top place among all Gods and among all peoples of the earth.

CHAPTER TWELVE:
CAUGHT IN ADULTERY
JOHN 7 AND 8

<u>Historical background and setting</u>

The year was approximately 25-30- A.D. Jesus was active in ministry in the city of Jerusalem at the time of the Feast of Tabernacles. The Pharisees were particularly concerned with his popularity among the people and the division that his presence created among them and the Jewish leadership. In the Gospel of John chapters 7 and 8 we see increasing turmoil in Jerusalem due to his public teaching and the confusion surrounding his identity. As the feast comes to a close, a group of Pharisees decide he must be arrested and questioned, so they dispatch several temple guards to bring him to the Jewish leaders. When this fails, they devise a plan to confront him and trick him into supporting a violation of the law, thus justifying an official arrest.

The Story

I am a Pharisee. I am an active member of the Jewish leadership body called the Sanhedrin, along with the only other religious party of influence called the Scribes. I work to insure that the sacred Law of Moses is upheld and honored by the people of Israel. Although we, as a nation, are officially under the rule of the Roman government and their military, we are allowed to oversee the religious and civic affairs of the nation in cooperation with the local Roman governor. We maintain a strict code of allegiance to the Law of God, His Holy Temple, the sacred City of Jerusalem and the many traditions of the our Jewish elders.

Because of this, we had great concern when this teacher from Galilee, named Jesus, who some claim has come as our Messiah, appeared among the people doing great signs and calling the nation to repentance. Most of us in the Sanhedrin group carried serious doubts about this man's credentials and had no patience for this nonsense concerning his coming as the Israel's Messiah. We had attempted many times to discredit this man and hopefully decrease his popularity among the people, only to be frustrated and see the whole of the nation caught up with intrigue concerning him. Now, as the Feast of Tabernacles was coming to a close, we made our move to trap him. This is my story.

I could feel the tension in the air as our great assembly met to discuss the matter of this Jesus of Nazareth. He had come to Jerusalem within the previous week as the Feast of Tabernacles was in full process. He came healing the sick and preaching the Kingdom of God with great boldness and his presence was stirring the people greatly and bringing suspicion upon us as leaders. We would not endorse this man, or at least, most of us would not endorse him and so thus, the official stance of the Scribes and Pharisees: public silence AND private resistance. So, the debate continued with strong emotion and argument. Some of our companion leaders actually seemed to support this so called Messiah, like Nicodemus, for example. Some encouraged patience and continued questioning to see whether or not his claims were legitimate. Most, however, including our High Priest, were angry and nervous with his popularity, along with his message that seemed to ridicule our traditions, expose our inconsistencies and make him out to be some prophetic fulfillment of the Old Testament promise of the Messiah.

Even as we met in our chamber and bantered back and forth across the aisle, Scribes on the one side and Pharisees on the other, reports were trickling in that this Jesus was in the temple complex calling people to follow him. At this latest word, a wave of disbelief rolled over the chamber. What was this itinerate preacher trying to do? Didn't he see the confusion he was creating and the awkward position he was putting us in as the nation's leaders? Without hesitation, in response to this latest provocation, the High Priest, Ananias, called for his arrest! Shouts of agreement rang across the room mixed with a few voices of descent urging restraint. Cooler heads did not prevail and the temple guards were quickly summoned. Through the maze of conflicting opinions, a group of them were sent to the temple to bring this man in for questioning.

As the guards left the room, we continued debating, arguing and jostling our opinions and doctrines against one another, hoping to come to some resolution that would bring calm to the city, order to our chamber and at the same time, preserve our coveted place of authority and influence. Soon the clamor dissipated and we simply waited for this mysterious man to arrive for our examination. You can imagine our consternation when after several hours had gone by, the guards returned WITHOUT him! They had gone to the temple courtyard and watched this Jesus preach, looking for an opportunity to apprehend him and bring him back, but could find none.

Each time they attempted to make their move they seemed to be stopped or held at bay by some invisible force that they could not explain. Whether it was the strength of his words or the tone of his voice, the energy in the crowd or some unusual combination of all these, they did not know.

They simply could not find a way to take him and thus had returned empty handed.

For the leaders of our esteemed group, this was unacceptable and their rage proved the point. The guards were accused of believing in this so called Messiah, as were a number of our own! Although no one among us would actually say the words, it was clear to me that our leaders knew that a subtle dissention was brewing in our ranks and they would not stand for it! Even though for some of us, seeing the guards with no prisoner was a relief, for others it was a disgrace. Regardless, for most it was now a prioritized reason to create a specific plan of attack.

The majority ruled! There did not seem to be any other way except to trap him in his own teaching, hopefully exposing what we thought was his disregard for the law and thus, finding reason to have him arrested. We simply needed a cause, a reason; a sensitive personal matter that would perhaps highlight the clear standards of the law, while enticing his message of mercy into a compromise. But, with no real solution presenting itself at this point, we could do nothing but adjourn for the day, reconvene on the morrow and hope that something would come our way to assist in our plan.

It was indeed very early on the next day that we saw our chance. As was the case on most days, our governing body would remain in session to review religious and civil cases, as well as respond to any issues the Roman governor, Pontius Pilate, brought to us. It was in this capacity that our opportunity presented itself. It came to us in the form of a young woman who was accused of adultery. Before the day had hardly begun, she was brought in by several temple guards, followed by several accusers, being partly dragged and partly lifted to the front of the court area. It was obvious by her tears, her loosely robed frame and disheveled appearance that she had been caught in the very act of her sin.

Every man in the room was instantly caught in his own emotional vise. On the one hand, the law screamed loudly for punishment of the most extreme kind; on the other hand, slight pangs of concern and mercy tugged at many hearts. While under this tug of war, the sight of this vulnerable and comprised woman sent feelings of both attraction and guilt through each man.

As we stared at this heap of feminine disgrace and being torn in our hearts by her appearance, the embarrassment of her story was told to us without any serious attempt to identify, who of course, should have been equally apprehended, charged and questioned. This uneasy atmosphere was interrupted when a suggestion was offered from one of the chief elders, much to the relief of the gawking men of the Sanhedrin. Would this not be the perfect issue to bring before our self-proclaimed Messiah? Could this decision be placed before him in the public arena and presented in such a way as to trap him? Indeed it could! So, just as the woman had been forcibly brought to us, she was quickly escorted out of the room and into the open air of the temple complex.

Several Pharisee brothers and I followed closely behind the woman and her escorts. I could see Jesus across the outer court just inside the Beautiful Gate entry. Already numerous people and disciples were gathering to listen to his teaching. This kind of gathering was a very usual occurrence as many rabbis and their followers would gather daily for teaching and discussion in the courtyard of the temple. One would see, almost daily, small scattered groups of men sitting with their mentor and teacher discussing matters of the law, as well as religious and political current events. So, even though we were disturbed by the following that this Jesus was encouraging, the setting was expected and in fact provided energy for our plan of attack to unfold.

Jesus sat on one side of a slowly enlarging circle with his disciples fanning out around him. This left an opening in the middle to provide adequate view for those watching and a close enough proximity to be able to converse with the teacher. Approaching this circle of gathered people from behind, we made our way through the seated followers of Jesus, dragging the young woman with us to the center of the group.

As she was thrust forward, still in her unkempt and unflattering wardrobe which suggested her previous night of promiscuity, her head hung in shame and although standing upright, her shoulders sagged and bent from the weight of her sin, betrayal and hopelessness.

"Teacher," the lead Pharisee began, "This woman has been caught in the act of committing adultery. The Law of Moses commands us strictly to stone such a woman. What do you say in a matter like this?" This whole line of thinking and questioning was of course designed to trap him and thus find some way to accused him of advocating disobedience to the law. With the proposal presented, we stood encircling the woman, watching this Jesus and waiting for an answer.

The people gathered around, whispered quietly among themselves, but the teacher said nothing. He seemed unimpressed and irritated by our interruption. In fact, rather than look up to us, he stooped to the ground and began writing in the dirt with his finger. The silence on his part and this peculiar response of dragging his finger through the dirt beneath him brought more persistent questions and pressure from our group of Sanhedrin leaders. What was his verdict? How would he apply the law to this woman's situation? Had he not understood the law's requirement for justice and holiness in such matters? Certainly, if he were a legitimate rabbi he could see the need for strong punishment in this matter, couldn't he?

With all of this questioning and harassment, Jesus simply continued to write with his finger in the dirt. As I watched this take place and pondered his odd response to our questioning, suddenly flashes of the scripture came to my mind. First, out of the book of Exodus, I could see the faint image of the finger of God engraving the words of the law on the tablets of Mount Sinai as the prophet Moses watched in amazement. Secondly, my mind traveled to the record of our people during their sojourn in Babylon. I saw flickers of mages of the hand and finger of God writing words of judgment on the wall of the palace of the King of Babylon.

These words of prophetic judgment were fulfilled as the Persian Empire captured the city and the King and his royalty were lost in a drunken stupor. This feeble writing in the dirt certainly could not be compared to those classic events in our history, could it? I tried fervently to rid my mind of such thoughts, even as the movement of this teacher's finger seemed to etch its way across the surface of my heart, as well as the dirt of the temple courtyard.

Finally, the teacher stood to face us, looking candidly into each of our faces and measuring our determination, he prepared to speak. Expecting a debate over the law and the circumstances surrounding this woman's sins, I was stunned by what I heard in his response. "The one without sin among you all should really be the first to throw a stone at her!" he said calmly and as a matter of fact to our group. Then, as if to complete his soil composition, he stooped again to the ground and continued his writing, saying no more and no less to us.

While this poignant interchange was taking place, people throughout the entire temple's outer court began joining the circle. Our commotion had the effect of adding to the crowd. Now, both Jesus and the Pharisees had a significant crowd to witness the results of this dramatic confrontation.

This had been exactly what we wanted to have happen and now I was not at all sure the results would be favorable to us. And to add to this uncertainty as well, something deep in my spirit had become uncomfortable with our original expectations! Nervous silence followed the words of the teacher from Galilee, as he returned to his earthly etching. The young women, now calmed from her earlier crying, still stood humbled in the center of the circle, the crowd looking intently at her predicament. We Jewish leaders, as well, stood awkwardly just outside of reach of the woman, yet still inside the circle of disciples and people in general, feeling the penetrating gaze of the curious throng that arched around and behind us.

The usual course of action in matters of this nature, would have been to wait for the woman's accusers to reach to the ground, pick up a stone and begin throwing it at the guilty party. Then, we the judges and the gathered witnesses who concurred with the verdict, would join the pelting of the woman until she would have been forced to the ground in pain or fatal injury or fallen unconscious from the blows of the stones to her head.

Then, with gruesome determination, we would have continued the onslaught until she was dead and left her lying in her own blood for family or some sympathetic person to carry her away. In this case, nothing of the sort developed! Instead, slowly, almost methodically and in humiliated fashion each of us who had self righteously presented the woman in the first place, turned to go.

We could only look for a quick exit from the circle, while fighting the pain of our own deep conviction. First, the older men drifted away, no doubt resolving their inner conflicts sooner that the rest of us. Then, the younger of us, whom I guess stayed longer out of our pride and zeal, did the same.

I had not only felt the pressure of this prophet's finger on my soul earlier in the episode, but now his words had struck me like a broad side jab in the gut, almost taking my breath away. I could only move as one in a kind of daze or fog to the outer edge of the circle of disciples and attempt to find a place to steady my feet and legs and somehow sort through what had just happen to us all.

It was then, in this place of deep reflection and convictive anguish that I looked back at the inner circle to watch this teacher address the broken woman who now stood alone. This Jesus had continued to write in the dirt, as the guilty leaders of Israel had filtered away one by one. Now he was standing up and looking directly at the woman. Addressing her softly, with gentle eyes and a probing stare, he said, "Woman, where are your accusers? Has no one remained to condemn you?" With head still bowed, her long brown hair draped down around her face and neck and still in disarray, she reply slowly, "No one, Lord."

In hearing this brief exchange, I too could only affirm the obvious. No one remained to condemn her. No one dared condemn her in light of what had just been said. Not only had the plan to trap this Jesus failed miserably, but the tool we had used so mercilessly in our effort had been lost as well. We, the illustrious leaders of God's people, had connived to dig a hole for the capture of this man and we had fallen in ourselves. We were the accused! We were the charged! We were the guilty and it was obvious to all that had been watching, including ourselves.

Now, with the lingering crowd beginning to disperse, Jesus only had one final comment for the relieved woman. "Then neither do I condemn you," Jesus said. "Go and from now on do not sin anymore." With those parting words, the Teacher departed, leaving the woman to her thoughts and several waiting female companions who rushed to comfort her and assist her in her new found freedom.

As for me, I could only stand frozen in my steps, my mind racing and stumbling to uncomfortable conclusions. I had begun this whole effort with a determination to expose the error and deception I believed was at work in this man's preaching, only to be left wondering out loud to myself, if indeed I had just seen the true Messiah at work!

DOUGLAS S. MALOTT

CHAPTER THIRTEEN:
JESUS HEALS THE PARALYTIC
MARK 2 AND LUKE 5

Historical background and setting

The year was approximately 25-30 A.D. Jesus had just begun his public ministry, called Simon Peter, Andrew, James and John as his first disciples and traveled into the area in the north of the Sea of Galilee to begin preaching. Apparently with Capernaum as his headquarters, he was traveling through the immediate area and then returning to the city for rest and resupply. By all indications, Jesus stayed in the home of Simon Peter and periodically hosted crowds of people for ministry and teaching at that location.

The Story

In the City of Capernaum was an anonymous paralytic who had suffered in his condition for many years. As news of the ministry of Jesus began to circulate among the people and reports of miracles continued to arrive with the migrating throngs of people, a plan was devised. The paralytic man would be taken by four of his closest friends to see the prophet, Jesus, and hope for a miracle for themselves. One of these friends in particular, who is himself unnamed and non-descript in the bible narrative, will tell us this amazing story of faith. Here is his story!

I had long lived in the city of Capernaum as a liveryman, working with both my fellow Jews and the Romans. The Romans were frequent visitors and residents in the city due to the strong military presence there. Over the many years, I had hoped that during our lifetime I would see the Messiah come to Israel, as did all of my countrymen. With the years fading slowly and many false prophets coming to disappoint us repeatedly, I did not find news of this Jesus of Nazareth to be so encouraging. I suppose one might say that my heart was a bit hard and calloused at being the target of so many deceived men. I just did not have the stomach to place my hope in another itinerating prophet. It was in this state of caution, and I suppose even suspicion, that I visited my good friend Aaron at his home next to my stable.

Aaron had long been paralyzed in both legs from a near fatal accident that had occurred long before I first knew him. In this sad condition he spent most of his days, sitting in his small one room lean-two shanty, doing little but a few odd jobs repairing leather goods and sandals for the local people. He had been born and raised in the city, so was known by most, but ignored by most, as well. He had no one to really care for him but his sister who visited every few days, trying to help with what she could in hopes of making life as easy as possible for him.

Although certainly better off than the local beggars and vagabonds, Aaron lived a meager existence due to his severe handicap and the general lack of interest on the part of the town's people toward him. I had felt sorry for him after doing business with him some years ago and had determined to help as best I could by visiting from week to week to assist where needed. It was during these weekly routines that he and I had soon become good friends. I also discovered, in this crippled twisted shell of a man, a deep and abiding faith. Although he certainly had every reason to be cynical and negative, he was not! He continued day by day to trust in the mercies of God and continually look for the hope of Israel when most around him did not.

It was in this vain that our conversation on one particular day turned to the matter of this Jesus of Nazareth and the reports we were hearing about his message and his miracles. Aaron was not as hopeful as I would have expected him to be in light of the things we were hearing about this Jesus. He, like many of us, had his doubts about another Messiah coming on the scene, although he admitted to me privately that he was trying to maintain an open mind. My response was simpler. I did not think that he was the Messiah, but perhaps I could give him room to be a prophet of some kind for the time being. What intrigued me more were the consistent reports of his healing power and the miracles that he was said to have performed. I told my friend, in the strongest of terms, that if these things were true, whether he proved to be a Messiah or not, it might be worth my effort to gather several additional friends together and try to get Aaron close enough for this Jesus to give him a miracle! What did he think about that? Aaron only sighed and looked at me with a kindly smile as if to say, "Don't worry about me, I'll be just fine!" I was not worried about my friend in the slightest; I knew that he would be taken care of by his sister and friends. I simple thought that if the stories about this Jesus were true, then what would it hurt to actually go and see him for ourselves. It was then and there that my plan took shape in my head. Although Aaron could not stand or walk and thus could not assist anyone trying to transport him to Jesus, I felt sure that two or three others along with me could make it work.

145

I simply had to wait for the right time. It seemed that Jesus and his disciples would travel in and out of the city on a regular basis, traveling into the outlining areas to teach and heal the sick and then returning home to rest. It would be during this rest period in the city that the best opportunity would be provided for us to act on our intentions. It was not long before news of his return reached us through several people who were making regular trips to hear him teach and, I am sure, to possibly watch him perform some miracle. Now, it seemed, was the right time for us to make our journey to visit this Jesus of Nazareth.

Three of my close companions and I arrived early to gather Aaron, a few of his belongings and travel to the home of Simon Peter. It was there, we were told, that Jesus was entertaining large crowds on a daily basis. A large cloth mat was placed on the ground at the door of Aaron's feeble home and with four strong sets of muscles, he was placed gently in its center. After insuring that our patient was comfortable, each of us grasped a corner of the mat and lifted it slowly, but firmly from the ground, moving away from his doorway and into the narrow street in front of us. The distance to Simon Peter's home was not great, but with the weight of our friend, the heat of the day upon us and the unkempt dusty road under our feet, the progress was slow.

Carrying our friend, we would walk some distance, stop, lower the mat to the ground, rest several minutes, raise the mat and then continue. This was our routine as we made our way over cobblestone and dust with the panoramic view of the Sea of Galilee to our left and the browning foothills beyond the city to our right. We were fortunate to have acceptable weather for the arduous trip and the gentle breeze of the water front helped keep us somewhat cool and refreshed during our rest breaks.

It was not long before Simon Peter's residence came into view. Expecting to need to wait our turn to see Jesus, we were prepared to find a cool place under a tree or next to a wall or simply to lower our friend to the ground and shade him ourselves, if needed. What we did not expect was the huge crowd that had arrived before us and was pressing its way into every open space it could find. People were standing or sitting everywhere. The doorways were full of people, the windows had people sitting in them and the main living room was so full it could hold no more! Stretching to my full height and looking forward toward the front of the crowd, all I could see was the top of people's heads or the back of their sweaty necks. People were blocking every pathway and avenue to the front where Jesus was now beginning to speak to the great assembly. We could hear him talking, but only faintly could we see him between the many heads and shoulders that stretched out ahead of us.

Looking back to my saddened companions, I could see the disappointment growing in their faces and knew instantly that we would have to have another plan or soon we would be plagued by our failure to follow through. Quickly I surveyed the residence standing before us and the few available access points around the outer wall of the home. The house of Simon Peter was a simple two story structure with the second story standing above only half of the home. The other half of the house was the common single story height that dominated most of the house's space. Inside the front entrance was a medium sized, but welcoming, courtyard with several smaller rooms, including the storage and kitchen areas attached in several directions around it perimeter. Like all houses in our city, the structure was made of carefully placed stones and mortar with interior walls of varying heights and a mostly flat roof made of long wooden beams covered with reeds, palm leafs or small branch slats that were in turn either covered with clay or layered tiles. In this case, however, there was a narrow stone staircase on the outside of the east wall that led up to the second story portion of the building. In a flash of adrenaline and faith I saw our answer!

Motioning to my companions to take up their mat corners, I reached down firmly, grasped my hand full of cloth and began leading the troupe around the back of the crowd to the exposed stairway. As we made our way along, I could periodically catch quick and fleeting glimpses of the Teacher in the courtyard through the house's small windows, viewing him briefly over heads and between bodies packed into the windows wells. These were so intensely watching and listening to the Teacher's words that they paid us little attention as we prodded slowly behind them. As we finally reached the first step upward on the stairs, the realization of what was in my head became obvious to the others. For just a momentary second, each of the three held their ground and stared at me with wide eyes. I simply looked down to our mutual friend, still clinging fearlessly to the mat between us, and started up the stairs. The others gathered their faith and their courage and fell in step alongside me.

Our rhythmic ascent was deliberate; up two stairs and then a rest stop, up three stairs and then another rest stop. With our final lift, we were brought to the top of the stairs onto a small porch or landing. If one could have taken the time, stopping to gaze back out over the lower houses and on to the wide blue expanse of the lake, it would have been a treasured moment. But as it was, we had no time to spare. My crippled friend and the other three partners now looked at me for further direction. Turning now back to the upper wall of the house, I carefully took a long slow stretching step and balanced myself onto the roof of the lower story of the house. This was done rather than entering the narrow door at the edge of the porch into the second story, which would be one's normal course of access on a normal day. But this day was not to be normal. My team, now full of their own adrenaline, saw where I was going and jumped at the chance to bring our crippled companion along with us. All five of us were going across the slender gap of space from the porch to the roof in no time. All of us making several stretching motions and hardy heaves to bring the mat and its needy cargo with it.

Once on the roof, we gently lowered the mat and our friend to the tile surface of the roof and started the unthinkable. Each of the four of us began lifting and removing tile after tile after tile to expose the dried reeds and thin branch framework beneath them. As each tile was set aside and the reeds and branches pulled apart and laid with the tiles, the open space below us began to come into focus.

First the faint sight of the tops of scores of heads, then a few of the furnishings in the room. Lastly, as a few last small bits of broken reed and branch and pebble fell floating, as if almost in slow motion, to the floor below, I could make out the head and face of the Teacher. He was looking up directly at us through the hole in the roof. It was then that the full magnitude of what we had just done and what we were about to finish came flooding into my mind. This great crowd of people from all areas of Capernaum and beyond was spellbound by this Jesus of Nazareth and we had just tore a hole in the roof the size of a man and interrupted the entire meeting! If it had not been the look of pleasure and joy on the face the Teacher, we might have abandoned our effort, but his face beckon us onward and seemed to applaud our daring strategy.

Now, with our last surge of physical strength, each of us, first kneeing on both knees and taking hold of our four corners of the mat and then lying flat on our bellies and extending out arms through the gaping hole, lowered our friend into and through the space just under us. Slowly and methodically, we gave each corner of the mat its fullest possible stretch, all the while dangling a hopeful, but crippled man down to the floor in front of the entire packed house. As the drifting dust and our straining, protruding arms and grimacing sweating faces were finally noticed by everyone under us, a flurry of shock and nervous talk and even laughter sprang from the now staring people. All of this reaction was the least of my concerns now. My only focus was on the face of the Master. Lying still on my belly and looking over the jagged edge of reeds and branches with still both of my arms dangling in the air under me, I only wanted one man's approval and that man was Jesus.

I'm not sure what I expected to hear the Master say after he took focus on my crippled friend Aaron and his crumpled mat. But, his words, "Son, your sins are forgiven," were a surprise! Apparently many others in the room were surprised as well, some even taken back by these words, because no sooner had I wondered about them, but Jesus questioned some in the crowd with a quick response. "Why are you thinking I am not allowed to forgive sins? Which is easier; to say to a paralytic, 'Your sins are forgiven' or to say, 'Get up, pick up your bed and walk?'" With that final comment, Jesus turned to my friend and commanded him, "I tell you, get up, pick up your mat and go home!"

As I listened to this exchange take place and watched my friend gazing into the eyes of this Jesus, I noticed immediately that the mat where he was laying began to quiver with the sudden jerking and twisting of Aaron's legs and hips which were still pressing against it. His thin bone-like feet, calves and thighs thickened with muscle, as the power of the Teacher's words settled upon his ears. Our friend, who had not walked in many, many years, was now being infused with strength right before our eyes. Each of my weary companions on the roof now recoiled in awe at what they were seeing. And, as our once crippled friend braced himself with one hand and then the other to stand to his feet, all three were making ready their descent of the stairs to meet him.

Aaron now stood erect in front of Jesus and everyone. Looking up and giving us a full glance and smile, he simply stood for several minutes enjoying his new view. The crowd now began to give glory of God and shout in astonishment having never seen anything like this happen before. Our friend, now with eyes full of tears, bent down, grabbed his mat with one hand and slung it over his shoulder never to be confined to it again! The crowd continued to buzz with amazement and awe at the sight of this spectacular healing. Our friend himself could not hold back shouts and proclamations of praise as he made his way through the press of people, who now touched, embraced and escorted him through the courtyard to the outside world of freedom and of course, his four friends who would soon join him on his walk home.

Before making our way off the roof and placing all the reed, branches and tiles back in place, I looked over the edge of the hole at the commotion on the ground level below and caught the Master looking up at us again with one final smile. The clarity and twinkle in his eyes seemed to commend us for our faith and tell us that he had approved our risky obedience and daring act of faith!

Now, gathering ourselves on the roof for our climb down the stairs, we could hear our friend calling to us from the ground and see him waving to us frantically, as he jumped and turned in small circles, testing his new limbs. It appeared to me that the four of us would have quite a walk home ahead of us!

DOUGLAS S. MALOTT

CHAPTER FOURTEEN:
THE TORN VEIL
MATT. 27:51; MARK 15:38; LUKE 23:45

Historical background and setting

The year was approximately 25-30 A.D. Jesus of Nazareth has been arrested, tried, condemned to die by crucifixion, and is hanging on the middle of three crosses on the Hill of Golgotha. A freakish darkening of the sky and an earthquake now accompany His final breath of life. As He dies and yields His spirit into heaven, a significant symbolic event takes place in the Hebrew Temple of God. The veil, separating the two inner rooms of the temple proper, is torn in two, from top to bottom, exposing the inner sanctum of the Holy of Holies, to the adjacent room, the Holy Place. This great Temple, which has been undergoing expansion and renovation for some 46 years at this point in history, is the center of religious life for all of Jewry. The ritual sacrifices and offerings conducted here were to be symbolic of the true eternal sacrifice made by God's Son on one needed final Passover Feast. As the true sacrifice takes place and fellowship potentially is restored to humanity, the symbolic separation represented in the veil is done away with in dramatic fashion. This monumental expression of the final work of the cross is witnessed by several unsuspecting priests.

The Story

A particular unnamed priest is preparing to fulfill his scheduled service in Herod's Temple, the Temple of God. As a priest and member of the Levitical family, he was assigned regular duties in the Temple to assist with daily animal sacrifices and maintenance activity in the Holy Place which housed three sacred items: The Table of Shewbread, the seven pronged Candelabra and the Altar of Incense. Careful daily upkeep was needed for all three furniture pieces as well as incense offerings made at the altar. This priest, after careful personal preparation, was going about his duties at the very moment that Jesus Christ died on Golgotha's hill. This coincidental scheduling forced him to witness something that would forever change his life. This is his story.

I am an anonymous character found in the pages of scripture, but what I experienced that day before Passover was anything but an anonymous event in history or in my life. Expecting nothing but the same routine and ritual maintenance of the sacred Temple of Jehovah, I found myself caught in the middle of God's final statement on the crucifixion of Jesus of Galilee. This story, although briefly stated in the scriptures, served to shake the normally safe and secure function of the priesthood for many years. This one event which I am about to describe to you brought a large numbers of priests to accept this Jesus as the Messiah, pledging to follow His teachings. I was one of those who faithfully practiced our strict adherence to the Law and the requirements for Temple service, but after witnessing the dramatic display of God's temple judgment became convinced of the truth of the Messiah's message.

This particular Passover season was no different than others I was involved in, except for the fact that the city was in an uproar over the presence and ministry of Jesus of Galilee. As one born of the tribe of Levi, I was commissioned to serve as a priest, as was expected of those from my family. After the commissioning, all priests were expected to draw lots for their placement in the regular cycle of priestly service in the Temple. This placement or 'course' would involve several weeks of work in the Temple, during which time each priest would travel to the Temple from his home town and stay in one of the many living quarters provided in the Temple complex. It was just such a commitment that I was performing as the entire nation of Israel approached its Passover celebration and simultaneously struggled with the sudden and dramatic arrival of Jesus into Jerusalem.

I had traveled from my home town of Bethlehem, about a two hour walk to the south of Jerusalem, making my way into the Temple complex. Entering from the west over the priest's bridge through the gate in the west portico, I had crossed the broad open Court of the Gentiles and slipped into the Priest's Court from the west at the back of the two inner sanctuaries. Finding a place in one of the small rooms along the narrow hallway which encircled the Holy Place, I had settled into my routine. A priest's undergarments, pants, tunic, robes, sash, and turban were provided as I began my stay in the Temple. Under no circumstances could a priest care for his own ceremonial outfit due to the need for strict adherence to cleanliness standards, thus I made my way to one of several storage rooms and secured my clothing, which had been cleansed and readied for me by other priests in the Temple. There was never a time in my years of serving in the Temple that I did not feel a keen sense of respect for my duties as I carefully dressed myself and proceeded to cleanse both hands and feet before beginning my duties. The snow white undergarments and robe, along with the small white turban, and the belt of woven blue and red, were worn with pride and a sense of holiness by all who served the Temple.

Upon dressing, I joined the others in my division and proceeded to draw lots for the many different duties and jobs that needed to be performed. With the Passover feast approaching, many more priests would be needed to assist in the sacrificial offerings brought in by the many thousands of faithful who would visit the Temple complex. I anticipated being selected for this gruesome and bloody duty, as it turned out, however, in a pleasant turn of events, my lot fell to the duties needed in the Holy Place. I would spend my Passover Feast days tending to the duties of the great hall that was situated just in front of the sacred veil! The Table of Shewbread, the seven pronged Candelabra, the Altar of Incense, and all the details concerning them, would be my focus for the upcoming holy days; a particularly inspiring privilege!

My quiet preparations for priestly duty were in stark contrast to the upheaval and strife that began early in the week before the Passover preparation. The teacher from Galilee had ridden into Jerusalem on a foal of a donkey and as he ascended into the upper level of the Temple complex, he set off a series of reactions that brought immense strife to our priestly leaders. Some of the priests, including myself, were open and sympathetic toward this prophet and teacher, but most were skeptical and suspicious of His messianic proclamations. There were some in fact, including several of the chief priests and the High Priest, that were incensed and angered at His ministry, and extremely jealous of the strong following He was garnering among the people. As the week progressed, I was hearing more and more rumors from the others priest who shared my duties that plans may be afoot to have this Galilean arrested. Talk in the inner chambers was that if it were possible for a clear accusation and guilty verdict to be obtained from the Sanhedrin, then the entire governing eldership was prepared to petition the Roman Governor, Pontius Pilate, to have this man punished and either imprisoned or executed. Such extreme effort seemed uncalled for in my opinion, but as it was stated to me by several of my co-workers, our leaders seemed to have too much to lose if this so called Messiah proved to be successful in His efforts.

Although troubled by the antagonism toward this Jesus, and the undercover plot to eliminate him, I attempted to simply keep my focus on the matters at hand. I was expected to help each and every day, and sometimes more than once in the same day, to attend the three sacred furniture elements in the Holy Place and see to it that each functioned properly.

The sacred, gold, seven-pronged Candelabra would need to be replenished with Holy oil periodically and the seven wicks trimmed to insure maximum burn, maximum light, and minimum smoke. The only visible element to be seen ascending in the room was to be smoke and aroma from burning incense NOT the candles!

Also, the sacred Table of Shewbread was to show, on a continual basis, twelve freshly baked loaves of bread, each representing one of the twelve tribes of Israel. So fresh loaves were brought each morning and arraigned along the top of the golden table, kept free of any unsightly elements like dust or insect. In fact, the great expanse of the hall, with its inlaid stone and dazzling wall coverings, was cleaned on a continual basis so as not to defile or contaminate the Holy atmosphere that stretched out before the great veil.

And finally, the sacred Golden Altar of Incense was to be kept clean and polished with fresh glowing embers provided continually, so as to supply instant sparkle, burning, and aroma when incense was sprinkled on its bowl shaped top.

Entering from the front entrance several times in a day's work and facing the great veil at the back of the Holy Place, I could see the Holy Table of bread on one side, and the Holy Candle with its flames flickering on the other. In the center of the room, just beyond the first two furniture pieces, was the Holy Altar standing in close proximity to the veil itself. This Altar, with its four cornered horns, stood continually offering incense before the Lord, and periodically would receive a flick or dab of sacrificial blood on each of its horns from the offerings taking place outside. The priest's courtyard directly in front of the entrance was a continual composite of shedding blood, burning offerings, and priestly activity. And I was never without awe and respect as I looked at this bloody provision for sin behind me, and then turning, would see the Holy Place extend before me. Its great scarlet veil at the other end reaching to its full sixty foot height in order to protect the Presence! The beauty, grandeur, pristine cleanliness, and holy atmosphere would at times take my breath away and release a rush of tears in my eyes, as I tried to fully comprehend the meaning of this awesome atmosphere.

With Passover now fully upon us, the busyness in the Temple and the several courtyards, increased dramatically around us. At the same time preparations were being made by the Roman military leaders to conduct a crucifixion just outside the western wall of our fair city. This was not entirely unusual, although, I was surprised that their intention was to start and complete the process of their execution before the arrival of the Sabbath of the Passover Feast. My surprise turned to sadness and suspicion when I discovered that one of the criminals to be tortured and killed was indeed the Prophet and Teacher from Galilee! The chief elders had apparently had their way and somehow convinced the Roman authorities that eliminating this possible Messiah was both necessary and beneficial. It seemed an exercise in hypocrisy to me for such qualified effort to be made simply because a few leaders were jealous of another man's success. It was then, that while standing in the spacious entrance of the Holy Place looking out over the rush of priestly duties before me, I thought of how ironic and coincidental the planned murder of this man from Galilee was to be.

He would be executed while the entire nation of Israel was slaying its paschal lamb and remembering the blood covering of the Exodus. Could that be significant? Did the timing of this execution mean anything on a larger scale? Was the deliberate action on the part of the High Priest and others actually a sign that this man from Galilee was more legitimate that they wanted us to think? I didn't really know, but something deep in my spirit was troubled by this parallel crucifixion AND Passover sacrifice! Turning and spinning slowly on my heels, I left the noise of bleating lambs and goats behind and stepped into the serene quiet of the first sanctum.

It was now preparation day before the Sabbath and we were preparing the Holy of Place for the evening sacrifice. This particular one was done only once a year at the Passover season. There would be NO blood taken into the Holy Of Holies at this time of the year, but a single spotless lamb would be selected for a pitiful destiny in the Priest's Court. It would be slain at the Burnt Altar of Sacrifice, where portions of its flesh would be burned, while some of its fresh blood would be captured in a sterile container and brought before the Altar of Incense, which maintained vigilance before the great veil. As the families of the nation of Israel killed their lambs and prepared their Passover meal, careful portions of this fresh blood would be touched to the top of each of the four corner horns of this altar, while incense of the evening offering was sprinkled into the burning, glowing, and requiring embers.

Again, by lot, I was chosen to be among the priests that would participate and witness this precise ritual. In the hours leading up to this final casting of incense on the fire, I had been required by my several duties to move in and out of the Holy Place, to and from the Priest's Court. The atmosphere in this outside arena had now become one of sharp tension. Without warning and without cause the entire sky over the city of Jerusalem had grown dark and sinister! From bright noon day sunshine, the heavens had darkened and turned to deep grey and black. There was no obvious sign of storms developing, just a lowering canopy of darkness. An eerie foreboding was being felt by many of us as we attempted to stay focused on our different tasks, but it was not easy, as the darkness continued throughout the whole of the afternoon.

It was, as I remember, about half way through the afternoon of dreary darkness that I was called back into the Holy Place for the culmination of the Passover celebration. Several of my co-worker priests and me stood silently as a senior priestly leader made his way down the center of the hall. In his hand was the small container of fresh blood, just delivered to him from the outside a few minutes earlier. I watched in reverence as this monumental act of solemnity played before me. The beautiful wall covering of scarlet cloth and upholstery muffled any intrusive sounds. With the greatest of care and ritualistic stiffness, he strolled quietly before us, his hemmed tunic providing the only sound as it swished and rubbed the stone floor below. Waiting for him at the Altar of Incense was another senior priest, standing ready with crystals and powder of newly mixed incense, being held in his open right hand. He was preparing to spread his treasure over the fire as the other priest touched fresh blood to the altar. Still in the room were the pleasant mixed smells of consumed oil from the Candlestick, scent of baked bread for the Table and the tell-tale aroma from previous splashes of incense on the coals of the Altar.

The great veil rose firm and rigid behind all of this activity. The two large hand embroidered prancing lions faced each other on the veil's surface, as if to mark the center spot of the great curtain, and the hidden glory behind it. Stretching the full width of the room, and being hung just below the ceiling above us, it draped downward just kissing the floors surface. From my place at the side of the room it seemed that the spectacular veil dominated the entire place, its formidable size and thickness pronouncing decisively that NO ONE could pass behind it and defile what lay hidden there. Whether it was just my sensitivity to the proceedings taking place elsewhere outside the city on Golgotha's hill and its accompanying blackness or something in the air in the very room where we stood, I wasn't sure, but I felt so strongly that both events were intrinsically tied together.

As many emotions and scattered thoughts trickled through my mind, I watched the blood gently touched to the altar, and then watched the sparkle, flashing, and popping of the incense as the flames reached upward to consume it even before it touched the coals.

It was then that everything changed forever!

Suddenly, without warning, the floor beneath us began to quiver! The wall coverings on either of the side walls began waving, first softly and then violently! The Table of Shewbread scooted and scraped against the stone floor as it was jostled from side to side! The Candlestick seemed to shudder under the seven flickering tongues of flame as it teetered! The Altar itself was pushed sideways and suddenly was at risk of toppling over, embers and sparks tumbling and rolling over the inlaid stones in the floor!

We were in the middle of an earthquake! The whole of the building was being shaken from its foundations, and in an instant, all of the serene and placid stability of the room was gone. Nothing was stable; nothing was untouched, everything within sight seemed on the verge of being damaged or destroyed. I was instantly caught in a panic of fear, as were the rest of the priestly servers. In order to not fall abruptly to the floor, I braced myself with one hand on the wall behind me, and slowly slipped to the floor, and then to my knees.

It was then that the unimaginable took place. The great veil of the Temple began to change shape right before our eyes. High at the top of the curtain, in the middle of its wide expanse, something was attempting to push through the thick tightly woven fabric. It appeared that huge fingers and knuckles were taking hold of the veil from the other side. Some invisible and celestial force from the glory of the inner room was now gripping the top of the veil. To the horror of all of us who watched, the four inch thick veil of separation began to tear and rip at the top with piercing sounds of snapping threads, bursting fibers, and separating strands of filament and string.

As if in half-time motion, the jagged edges of torn veil continued appearing further and further down the full length of the scarlet hanging. The whole veil was being torn in two! The one piece was now becoming two, as the terrible sound of dividing material continued! It was not until I could see into the black space in the upper reaches of the Holy of Holies, through the fast appearing split in the veil that my now pulsating fear and shock turned to absolute dread. This giant supernatural force behind the veil was going to expose the inner sanctum. The veil of separation would no longer hide the Divine Presence! Whether an angel sent from God or the Lord Jehovah himself was responsible, at this point it did not matter. Within a matter of just a few seconds, The Presence of Unspeakable Holiness and Glory would be open to the outside world. This thought almost seared my brain with its potential. What would take place as this happened? Tradition told me that no one saw the Lord's Presence and lived! There could be no melding of human worthlessness and the Perfection of God. In a confrontation such as that, the man would be consumed and the Glory left untouched!

The Holy Place was now empty of its priests, except for me. Everyone had made their exit by any means possible, whether running, crawling, or staggering, they were determined to escape the horror unfolding before them. If the earlier freakish darkness had not been enough, and the earthquake that seemed to be centered right under us didn't do it, certainly seeing the great veil tearing from top to bottom had been the final straw that sent them all scrambling for their lives.

Still kneeling against the side wall in the eerie stillness of the torn veil, I now became aware of the strong pounding in my chest and head from a heart and mind that were both completely overwhelmed. No words would rise to my throat. Breath could be found but forming it to make sounds proved fruitless. I was dumb struck and numb from what I had just seen. I could do nothing but slide awkwardly to the stone floor and sit motionless staring at the still gently swinging pieces of veil. One breath at a time, I slowly calmed my soul and composed my thinking enough to assess the condition of the room. None of the furniture had fallen but each of the sacred pieces was uncharacteristically perched in unfamiliar places in the room. Some faint incense smoke could be seen wafting upward and being pulled into the space behind the split veil, as the air currents were slowly sucked into the gloom behind the broken hanging cloth. Looking back at the entrance, I could see through the opening left from the one door panel that had not been shut in the panic that took place earlier. I could see that the sky was fast becoming bright again. That awful gloominess that accompanied the death of Jesus, the Prophet, was lifting.

Now, gaining enough strength to move, I leaned my weight against the wall and pulled one leg and then the other up under me to be able to stand. From my standing vantage point, I could see into the Holy of Holies and noted that it was still, quiet, dark, and empty. Although I had a very fleeting thought of stepping to the opening and looking fully behind the veil, I could not bring myself to do so. Still, the dread of looking into that sacred place without atonement blood as my shield, gripped my heart. Slowly and mechanically I stepped to the entrance of the Holy Place to leave, each step being taken with a grimace and a brief holding of breath, wondering if the Majesty of God would rush to me and strike me down in judgment. But it did not! With each step taken I sensed a lifting in my spirit, a wave of tranquility surge into me, and a strong assurance of God's mercy gird up my mind. Stepping through the double doors out onto the entry porch, I looked one more time back toward the veil. It no longer separated God from His people; it no longer posed a barrier to The Presence! It was a relic to a past glory that somehow seemed empty.

Turning now to the brightening sky which illuminated the beautiful city of Jerusalem, I looked out over the courtyard. The sacrificial activity had come to an abrupt halt. It appeared that much of the offering animals and attending rituals had been interrupted and left unfinished by both fleeing patrons and priests. Only now were a few fearless people making their way back to where they had left their previous duties and obligations, attempting to make some sense of the whole bizarre afternoon. Just before taking my own final steps down the wide entry stairs to my sleeping quarters, I rehearsed the uncanny demonstrations that had taken place over that last three hours. It seemed that they had paced and paralleled the crucifixion and death of Jesus of Nazareth.

I did not know the exact moment of His death since

I was preoccupied with attending the Passover offering by the chief priest. I only knew that the earthquake had struck and the veil had been torn at the precise moment of the Passover incense and blood offering. It had been as if the realms of the unseen had reacted to the priest's actions. As if somehow there was more happening than just a sprinkle of blood and powder on the fire. I wondered if I would learn later that Jesus had passed into glory at the exact same moment as the Temple's sacrifice was offered. I wondered if this death was just an ordinary one or perhaps much more. I wondered if this death had caused all of heaven to recoil and vent its anger on a sacred veil that now could not hide God. I wondered if this man from Galilee was indeed all He had claimed to be and if so I wondered what would happen next.

CHAPTER FIFTEEN:
THE GERASENE DEMONIAC
MARK 5; MATTHEW 8; LUKE 8

<u>Historical background and setting</u>

The year was approximately 25-30 A.D. Jesus of Nazareth had just finished ministry in the area of the City of Capernaum with His disciples, along the northwest shore of the Sea of Galilee. They had crossed the Sea to the Southeast and arrived in the region of the Decapolis, so named for the ten cities that dominated the area. Of these ten cities, one was the City of Gerasa, situated in the hill country of the Jordan River valley. About a two day journey from the shores of Galilee to the east, it was the sight of a very dramatic deliverance at the hands of Jesus the Christ. A man whose life had been plagued and controlled by demons for many years, and whom the local people had driven out of their city due to his extremely unstable mental capacity, lived among the tombs and burial sites just outside the limits of the city. Jesus would arrive with plans to itinerate in the area, but would have those plans changed as He and His disciples are met by this savagely demonized man.

The Story

I am a living miracle! Having been healed by a single word spoken from the Messiah's gracious lips, I now live in the Decapolis area of Palestine and am able to give witness and proof of His power and message. Those who know my story are amazed at the change they see, having watched my insanity for many years.

Not too many years ago, I was a hopeless, mentally crazed demoniac, whose daily routine consisted only of moment to moment tortured efforts to survive. Each day was given to extreme mental anguish, hours of chasing voices that taunted me from the inside, terrifying the local people with my wrath, attempting to scrounge what little food I could find along the way, and repeated cycles of self mutilation. I was doomed to this constant mental and physical torture and no doubt would have eventually taken my own life had it not been for a monumental encounter with the Messiah. This is my story.

The Decapolis was a geographic area to the east of the great sea consisting of ten cities with rich Greek heritage and strong Roman influence. For the most part the people in the area lived a simple life, and although there were many poor people, by in large the area prospered well. This was not the case for me. My home for many years was a local grave yard. It was the only place that brought any semblance of calm to my spirit. It seemed that friendship with dead men's bones, burial tombs, and grave markers was my best choice, since life with the living only agitated greatly the powers of evil within my soul. I had long since been rejected and abandoned by the people of Gerasa who had no recourse against my demon inspired hate and rage. The city people had tried to contain my fits, hysterics, and convulsions, but with little success. Even their chains and metal shackles were useless against my fury. In a fit of foaming frothy wrath, I could snap chains as if they were dry reeds, and crush ankle and wrist shackles like pottery, screaming at my would be captors with bellowing voices that were not my own.

This happened on numerous occasions and had left nothing that could be done for me by the local people, their only recourse being to chase me from the city with clubs and sticks and leave me to the wild animals. I was a demonic vagabond, a haunted demented urchin, with nothing for which to live.

Having no friends or family that would claim me, my only companions were demons, my only conversations were with spirits of torture, and fear that daily kept my soul raw with rage. I lived in constant turmoil and mayhem of mind. Arguments, wild urgings, and circular nonsensical debate would constantly rise and fall in my thinking, blocking my ability to clearly perceive reality. During the day I would endlessly and uselessly roam the mountains and lonely hills seeking to find a safe place to hide from my invisible attackers. I could find none! Not knowing, of course, that the danger I was fleeing from was inside of me. In the night hours I would make endless journeys and circular wanderings through the shadows of the grave yard howling and growling at anything that moved, as well as the bickering vocal tones that echoed over and over in my mind.

In this complete state of dark control I ate next to nothing, could not bathe or clean myself, wore tattered and torn garments, and was covered from head to toe with dirt and mud and my own excrement from repeated cycles of rolling and squirming on the ground. This was done in many feeble attempts to rid myself of the pain of demon claws and teeth that gripped and stabbed and tore at me from within. From the lonely view of my hollow heart, looking out on a frightening world, I could see only a world of blackness and gray. Colors were mostly faded to neutral and the beauty of nature was invisible to me since I was only motivated by pain, anguish, torture, and the driving pressure of my hellish partners who constantly mocked me.

Eventually I was left with little to do but take sharp and jagged stones to my hands, arms, legs, and face hoping that the physical pain of cutting and stabbing myself would hide the inner pain. It did not, and I was left with only a deeper fiendish taunting.

It was from this crazed condition of mind, that one day, I ventured to lift my head and cast my hollowed eyes over the valley below that opened westward toward the Sea of Galilee. Groaning with ominous sadness, I turned my attention away, just briefly, from the cold stony surface of my favorite grave marker, which I held on to for hours on end hoping the cool touch on my skin would distract my mind. My brief glance brought into focus in the distance a group of people making their way up the valley from the lake. These were traveling toward the junction road that led from the tombs to the city. Travelers of this kind were not unusual and many times I would watch them while crouched among the tombs, and then suddenly howl at the top of my lungs as they passed by me toward the city. Frightening them I am sure but thinking in my contorted mind that they were intruding upon my space. At other times I was known to have run screaming into the road attempting to grab food or clothing pieces only to be driven off with rods or sword or spears.

On this particular day, as I gazed down toward the valley road, something inside of me suddenly gripped my insides with groaning and yelps of pain! The many voices already conversing in my head now shouted in my spirit and were instantly agitated, disturbed and troubled by someone in that group of people walking toward me. Incredible fear rose violently in my heart and every inner personage seemed to be straining to discover who or what was moving up the road toward me. Almost every fiber of my being wanted to run and hide, to find an open tomb to fall into, or just disappear into the mountains again. But also, deep in the forgotten recesses of my spirit, something else yearned to meet these people, something in me was drawn to these visitors; something in me had to identify these strangers to my grave yard!

Before my mind could fully grasp the emotion and passion that now surged through my body I was off at a full run, out from among the grave markers and down to the valley road to meet these visitors. Running at full speed;

stumbling at times, crawling at times, and panting with the sounds of a wild animal I moved head on toward the group. Through my wide crazed and bloodshot eyes I could not see the group beginning to defend themselves from my approach. I only heard inner growling and hissing along the way as I was aiming for the man in the middle with the full length white robe. Something in my mind, like a homing signal, pressed me toward him. Coming to within a few inches of the edge of His garment I fell to His feet, gnawing my teeth and gums and tongue while physically twisting and convulsing. The demons inside of me made every attempt they could to lean as far away from this man as possible.

Those who were standing around this man gasped and recoiled as they watched me writhe in front of them. Looking up at their reticence, from my pathetic position on the ground, I somehow knew they were justified in their reaction! The man in the white robe, however, neither recoiled nor gasped. He simply knelt down on one knee, looked directly into my eyes and said, 'Come out of this man, you unclean spirit!' At the sound of His powerful words I wanted to stretch out my hand toward Him and appeal for help, but before I could even finish the thought I was forced to listen as a chorus of inner voices pleaded for their lives. Distorted, twisted, shrieking voices poured out of my mouth, 'What do You have to do with me, Jesus, Son of the Most High God? I plead with You before God, don't torment or destroy me!'

I had not seen this man before, knew nothing of His ministry and calling and had no idea why He was here just outside the entrance to my grave yard! But those who lived and brooded in me knew exactly who He was and were instantly in fear for their pathetic lives! Their revulsion was linked directly to the divine nature of this visitor!

In all my years of torment, I had not been made aware of the extent of my own demonic trouble. These whom had possessed my mind, soul, and body had purposely kept a dark covering over my thinking. At first, blaming those who were around me, they justified THEIR control and MY anger. Next, blaming me, they turned their hatred toward me and prodded me into self-destructive actions; and lastly, mocking my very life and existence, they pounded my mind into total submission to their destructive motives and plans. I was helpless against them not knowing until the very moment of this confrontation that literally thousands of demonic entities had been living in my soul!

As I continued to lie squirming in the dust, the Man in the white robe continued His conversation, 'What is your name?' He asked. 'My name is Legion,' the voices inside me answered Him, 'because we are many,' they smirked. Looking up into the eyes of this Man brought both fear and relief to me. I could hear the conversation but could not respond; I simply lay at His feet drawing upon His mercy! As this Man stared into my soul with more and more authority, the voices of the thousands of grotesque spirits began to cry out again with their tortured and screeching voices, 'Don't send us away!' 'Please allow us to stay in this land!' 'Send us...to the pigs!

Pigs? I had not known any herd of pigs was in the area! The unclean nature of these animals did not allow an orthodox Jew to maintain such herds, so as it was, few herds were to be seen in this region and only then when raised by gentiles. With my demonic distraction in full force I could not notice the herd of pigs being mentioned. I only knew that the Man in the white robe was commanding my vision now and so all I heard was the raspy voices of the demons screaming out of me in reaction to His stare. The black terror that boiled in me brought the pulling and pinching of their presence in my spirit to a heightened level as they attempted to hold onto their place and not let go.

With one word this legion of evil spirits was commanded to go. This Man in the white robe, who looked directly into my soul, spoke once and spoke firmly and instantly a rush of dark energy began shooting from my inner man and seemed to empty from every cell in my body. My ears were filled with the sound of screeching screams of defeat and my body quivered and shook as an unknown but beautiful force seemed to suck the presence of evil out of me and discharge it toward the hillside in the direction of the pigs. Vaguely I could make out the shadow of this Man of power and His companions standing over me ready to assist. In the background now, with my hearing returning to normal, I was beginning to hear faintly in the distance the sharp squealing noise of a couple thousand head of swine frantically stirred into a rampaging stampede. The sound of this demonized stampede was only muffled into silence by their deathly plunge into the Sea of Galilee.

The silence in my mind startled me! I could not remember a time when I did not have screaming voices railing on the inside of my head. The serene calmness in my spirit felt like I was suddenly surrounded by a placid lake of unendingly smooth water. I could hear and see clearly and think with my own thoughts without interruption or confusion. The previously gray shades that dominated my view of life were fading now, being replaced with splashing, exploding spurts of color and bright hues. I was almost overwhelmed by the return to sanity. I found myself gazing out toward the hills, down over the valley, and then back to my own steady hands and arms, not being able to remember a time when I could sit quietly and enjoy such splendor. I glanced momentarily to the many faces staring down at me and then back again to my own peaceful body, amazed at the transformation taking place.

Before I knew fully what was happening to me, I was brought fresh water to drink, its coolness for the first time actually refreshing my mouth and throat. Additionally, water was brought to provide a cursory attempt to wash. Although not near enough to make a complete cleansing, it started on the outside what had been done totally on the inside. With a borrowed tunic passed to me by one of the bystanders, the stench covered and tattered pieces of cloth I had used for my clothing were replaced. I sat clothed, in my right mind, and awaiting instruction from the One whose word had set me free.

After a few minutes of sitting and watching the visitors around me, I became aware of a growing number of people who had slowly gathered from the surrounding countryside. These were here apparently because they had caught glimpses of the original meeting and exorcism and wanted to discover more about what was happening. Also, as was evident over the next hour or so, the herder of swine had returned from his panicked retreat earlier with several large groups of people from town who were arriving to assess the truthfulness of his report.

As many of the local people soon realized they were observing the crazy man from the tombs, who now was sitting before them completely sane, they began to bristle with fear! Confused comments and scattered conversations of inquiry only served to bring the fright and concern more to the forefront. Soon, eye witnesses began describing the scene they had observed previously, telling of the confrontation between me and the Man from Galilee and the deliverance that had followed. They also recounted the freakish insanity among the pig herd and their destruction as they plunged down the steep bank of the shore into the water below.

The fear and confusion that hung over the crowd became more resistant as the details of the events became clearer to everyone. It was not my newly found sanity that appeared to put these people off, but rather, the works of this Man in the white robe had struck at the heart of those who conversed with us. The presence of one who controlled demons, freed the demonized and transferred evil possession from man to beast was not wanted in this region!

Soon the entire throng of people was begging this Man and His companions to leave. I did not want Him to go! How could I wish for such a thing! This Man had come as a stranger and visitor to our shores and ended up being a deliverer! And He had delivered me! I certainly did not want Him to leave, in fact, I hoped that He would stay and continue His miraculous work in our cities. But, the single voice of a once frenzied demented homeless man carried no weight. The crowd was insistent; these travelers were not wanted!

The Man from Galilee and His companions slowly turned in the direction in which they had come, and proceeded to their sailing vessel, which awaited them on the rocky shore of the lake. Several of the local people followed along to ensure their departure but could not keep me from running through the scattered few people who were left and approaching this Man in the white robe and His followers. If the people of the area were not willing to welcome them, then I did not want to stay. I wanted to join this companion group and follow this Man as well. In fact, I insisted on climbing into the ship and sailing away with them, but this Man from Galilee would not allow it, He instead had another plan for my zeal and passion. 'Go back to your own people', He instructed me. 'These need to hear how much the Lord has done for you and how He has had mercy on you', he concluded!

There was no arguing in this matter. I stood placid and still as these wonderful visitors climbed into their vessel and pushed off from the rocky shoreline. Still feeling such yearning to follow this Man, I stood watching for some time as the ship grew smaller and smaller on the lakes horizon and eventually moved out of sight.

Most of the previously gathered throng of people had now dissipated and disappeared into the surrounding countryside. I alone was left at the water's edge, with the words of the now departed Messiah still echoing in my mind. Back to my own people I would go!

Turning away from the water and looking up the valley toward the hills, I knew that I would never be the same again and indeed needed to return to those who knew me best and explain to them why! As this day continued toward the night, I would now walk past the tombs and grave markers, having no attachment to them now. I would walk the valley road into the city, watching the mountains and hills but having no compulsion to run into their once dark hiding places. Leaving my former life behind me and traveling on into the city, I would bring word and testimony of my healing and then watch as family, friends, and acquaintances marveled at my appearance and report, hearing first hand of the work of the Messiah!

CHAPTER SIXTEEN:
HEALING THE ISSUE OF BLOOD
MARK 5; MATTHEW 9; LUKE 8

<u>Historical background and setting</u>

The year was approximately 25-30 A.D. Jesus the Messiah was in the beginning stages of the public ministry and drawing a crowd everywhere He went due the miracles he was performing. Having just returned from a brief stop on the east side of the Lake of Galilee, Jesus and His disciples returned to the area surrounding Capernaum and were immediately greeted by crowds of curious and needy people. Two of them, Jairus, the leader of the local synagogue, and an anonymous woman who had suffered many years from a debilitating issue of blood, were among the seekers. Each of them sought an audience with Jesus but each would approach their task in very different ways.

<u>The Story</u>

I am an anonymous character in the New Testament, a woman of Hebrew decent and heritage. Having lived in the area of the city of Capernaum and the great Lake of Galilee all my life, I was well known to the people of my village. My notoriety was due, however, to my unusual and repulsive illness. This illness and its effects kept me at a distance from people I loved and people I needed. It was in this desperate condition that I made my way to this Jesus of Nazareth and found more than I could have ever imagined! This is my story!

Being a woman in Israel made for many daily challenges. We were expected to care for our families and maintain our meager homes as well as engage in work and service, if possible, to supplement our families' existence and prosperity. As if this were not enough, we were strictly limited in our ability to serve in any political manner or religious manner as well. To add insult to injury, in my condition, I was isolated and rejected by most respectable people. I was unclean!

Some twelve years prior to this time I had become sick with a mysterious illness that robbed me daily of energy and life. Without any warning, after one of my regular monthly cycles of menstruation, I had found that I could not stop a flow of blood that apparently was issuing from an internal hemorrhage of some kind. I did not know the cause or the cure. Each month I would suffer for days on end with slow continual bleeding, dull aching pain, and cramping as a result of this disorder. I would find myself forced to remain in bed or drastically limit my ability to do the simplest of duties or chores. As the first months passed I maintained hope of getting well and regaining my strength but, as the malady continued, I began to sink into repeated bouts of despair and depression. I soon was losing hope that I would ever be able to return to a normal life.

As word of my condition spread through the village, I was first greeted with concern and care. People were sympathetic toward my plight. But after the months eventually turned into years, I was ultimately treated with disdain and rejection due to the fear and foreboding that surrounded my continued disorder. What was an added burden to my plight was the detachment that was forced upon me by our Hebrew religion.

You see, continued unchecked bleeding, such as I was experiencing, was seen much like leprosy and treated the same way. The stigma of continued sickness and the unknown nature of the bleeding made me 'unclean' in the eyes of the law and thus forced me to keep my distance from the people around me.

Over the years I had spent much time attempting numerous remedies prescribed by many doctors, all to no avail; in fact, there was evidence that in the months prior to meeting this Jesus of Nazareth, my condition had been worsening. The sacrifice of time and money which I had made to find a cure left me emotionally and spiritually empty. As well, I had only the barest of provisions for daily living given the fact that I had spent my life savings on the effort. And on top of all of this, I faced embarrassment and humiliation on a daily basis when forced to cry …'Unclean, unclean'… as I attempted to make my way through my daily routines.

It was in this daily condition of suffering that I first heard about the man who some called the Messiah. I was not sure of this Man's qualifications. Though I did not know whether He was to be our much needed and longed for Messiah, the reports of His ability to work great healing miracles intrigued me. Many had brought good reports back from Capernaum, as well as the lake country, concerning His teaching and authority. Others had said He commanded demons and spirits! Some had witnessed the lame and blind healed by simply a touch or a word from this Man. A few, who were fisherman, had brought reports back to us that this Man could even command the storms and the seas!

Was this indeed the promised Messiah? Was He a Prophet sent from God to bring a word to the nation? Or perhaps He was an up and coming political leader who would soon challenge the existing system and usher in again the government of God. These were all thoughts that rumbled through my mind, and the minds of others, as news spread of this Man's special message and power.

After several weeks of hearing such glorious reports

and stories concerning this Jesus, I was aroused from my groggy and lethargic afternoon sleep to hear that this Man of healing was nearing our village. The reports from my neighbors stated that He and His disciples were being mobbed by a huge crowd of people, near the market place, all wanting to be touched or prayed for while He was passing through. At first thought, I was compelled to ignore this visitor and simply remain wasting away on my sick bed. But the more I thought, the more I pondered, the more I prayed, the more I became stirred about the possibilities of meeting Him. The more I contemplated my dilemma, the more I knew, that I had to make the effort to find him and do whatever it would take to get close to this would be Messiah.

It was all I could do to muster enough strength and energy to get to my feet, the loss of blood sapping me of stamina and endurance. Entering the outside world was a frightening prospect for me, given my condition and its unaccepted stature in our culture. Several times I hesitated, while making my way through the doorway, toward the bright possibilities of the day that was in full expression beyond my front gate.

Something, however, urged me onward in spite of every hint of stopping. I decided I would not let fear or embarrassment keep me from finding this Man of power; I forced my way forward. In light of the stigma of my condition I elected to take along extra head coverings and shoulder wraps to help conceal my identity. And given the rejection I would face if I called out my uncleanness, I chose to remain quiet and secretive so as not to create a scene or become an embarrassment to this Man from Nazareth.

Once outside and walking slowly toward the market place, I caught site of the large press of people moving at a snail's pace as they swarmed around the Prophet and His disciples.

People reached in every direction trying to close the gap between themselves and this Man of healing. The narrow walkway through the vendor's tables and small carts and wagons left little room for maneuvering. It appeared to me that His followers, His close companions, were making every effort to protect Him from the frantic emotion and zeal of the people who desperately wanted to see Him, talk with Him or simply touch Him. Watching this jostling of people ahead of me brought fear to my heart at first as I contemplated how I might squeeze through the compact arraignment of bodies that were all reaching to the same Man. But with no hope to be found anywhere else for my predicament, I only became more determined in my heart, as I pondered how I might access this Man in the center of the crowd.

Moving slowly between people, squeezing, pushing, and prodding, I inched ever closer to this Jesus. At last, moving to within an arm's reach of His back, I could see that His disciples were not letting anyone close enough to touch or embrace Him. I knew instantly that they would not let me approach Him in any formal way; I had no choice but to lower myself to the ground and attempt to crawl the final few feet toward Him. With pain and squeamish sensations rushing through my stomach and legs, I slipped quietly to the dirt below me, leaned forward on my hands, and began pulling each throbbing knee and lower leg forward. I started crawling slowly along to keep up with the sluggish movement of the throng. Closer and closer I made my way toward the Healer. All I could see immediately in front of me and to each side, from my vantage point, were ankles, dirty feet, sandals, and lower edges of hanging tunics and robes of every size and color. The one I had my focus on, however, was the white one that hung straight and true without seam or stitch.

At last I was within reach. There was no time to waste. If I did not act now the crowd would move on and I would be forced to crawl further on my ever weakening legs and knees. Reaching with one great strong effort I told myself, as I stretched my hand and arms out in His direction, that if I could just touch His robe, grasp the edge or a corner of His garment, I would be made whole. Even as I reached I could feel the flow and movement of blood in my clothing, as the strain of walking through the market place, pressing against the people, and now creeping along the ground, had severely aggravated my wounds. But reach I did and as my feeble fingers extended out and I felt the soft smooth fabric of His robe, something strong and invisible shot back at me.

From the tip of my finger, down through my hand, down my arm, and then into my entire body, a surge of power, energy, and strength was released! I had not expected that to happen! I was not sure what was going to happen but I was not expecting something of His virtue to transfer into me! I slumped momentarily back on my haunches and both knees and just remained still, relishing the sensation that was now spreading downward to my stomach and womb. In the midst of the warmth and heat that I was now feeling I could tell that my bleeding had stopped. A gentle firmness, a sensation of solidity, and relief told me that the debilitating flow of my precious life blood had stopped. It was now at an end! The liberation was almost overpowering. The absence of pain and discomfort was almost intoxicating. Twelve years of suffering was gone with just one touch of this Man's garment. Warm tears of joy were now cascading down my cheeks, dropping in slow motion to my garment, and to the dust below.

I was healed! I was really healed! Every fiber in my body echoed my cry! I was healed! The enjoyment of my relief was interrupted suddenly when above me in the crowd I could hear the Man of healing questioning those around Him. 'Who touched my robe? He questioned as He turned in my direction. Several of His disciples reacted to His inquiry with disbelief. With this amount of people pressing in on all sides of Him, of course, someone might touch His robe! It seemed to me that His disciples were surprised by His comment and unimpressed by such a simple observation.

I could see that He was not to be denied. He still was insisting on knowing who had touched His robe, and it seemed to me that He knew, somehow, that some kind of power had been released from His person. My tears of joy now turned to tears of trembling and fear. What would He think of me for intruding upon His journey? Would He be angry at me? Had I violated His personal space? Was this surge of healing power that I felt not available to just anyone?

Rising ever so slowly, so as not to make a scene for the others, I moved directly in front of this Man of God and dropped again to my knees, crying out my tale, and making confession to the journey of faith that had led me to make my lunge and touch His robe. I explained ever so clearly that the touch of His garment had resulted in my healing and a complete stoppage to my bleeding condition. I poured out my story with emotion and tears hoping to defer any anger or rejection He might have toward me. But there was none! This Man from Nazareth draped in His white robe and simple blue sash only stared at me with loving eyes. His full tall frame, highlighted by His dark wavy hair, neatly trimmed beard, and broad smile only welcomed me with His gaze. 'Daughter,' He spoke to me softly, 'your faith has made you well today.' 'There is no need to be afraid', He continued with a smile, 'Go in peace and be forever free of your affliction.'

I could not find words to express my overwhelmed heart at that moment. I simply continued my joyful crying and stood silently watching as this Man of healing, who just might be the promised Messiah, turned to join His disciples. As the crowd began to fully absorb the impact of my testimony of healing, it was reinvigorated and energized again toward this Man and continued its press around Him as He moved away from me. Through the market place, on toward the synagogue beyond, it moved, as I simply whispered a quiet word of thanks toward this Man, and taking a full deep painless breath, turned toward home.

DOUGLAS S. MALOTT

CHAPTER SEVENTEEN:
JESUS AND JAIRUS' DAUGHTER
MARK 5; MATTHEW 9; LUKE 8

Historical Background and Setting

The year was approximately 25-30 A.D. Again, Jesus the Messiah was in the beginning stages of the public ministry, and drawing a crowd everywhere He went, due to the miracles He was performing. Having just returned from a brief stop on the east side of the Lake of Galilee, Jesus and His disciples returned to the area surrounding Capernaum and were immediately greeted by crowds of curious and needy people. Two of them, Jairus, the leader of the local synagogue, and an anonymous woman who had suffered many years from a debilitating issue of blood were among the seekers. Each of them sought an audience with Jesus but each would approach their task in very different ways.

The Story

My name is Jairus. I am a Jew and a religious leader in the City of Capernaum. As a synagogue leader I was responsible for conducting weekly Sabbath meetings in our local place of worship. I would regularly select those who were to lead the prayers, read from the Holy Torah, and preach in the hallowed chambers of our blessed synagogue.

Our first century synagogue was a beautiful stone structure with elegant columns and spacious stone-paved meeting areas. I was proud of our graceful place of worship, and faithfully led our people in their practice of Judaism.

At the time that Jesus of Nazareth began actively preaching in our region, I was able to hear Him speak only on a couple of occasions, and after assessing His strong pointed message, was not sure how to respond to this very outspoken Teacher. It was not until my daughter became gravely ill that my attention was drawn solely to this Man, His message and dramatic healing powers being the only hope for my daughter's life. This is my story.

I had been a very contented leader in Judaism. For the most part, the Roman government had not intruded into our practice and style of worship, leaving us great freedom to govern our own affairs, remain faithful to the requirements of the Jewish Law, and hold regular public meetings to honor Jehovah. In the duties that required my attention for the synagogue, I had been exposed to the teachings of this Jesus of Nazareth. In the early days of His public ministry, after relocating to Capernaum from Nazareth, He had faithfully attended our Sabbath meetings and on occasion spoken to those of us present. His message of repentance and the coming of God's kingdom brought sharp division to our leadership and great curiosity to our people. As His demonstrations of healing and absolute power over demons increased among the people, many began proclaiming Him to be the promised Messiah. As a synagogue leader and student of the law and the prophets of our sacred scripture, I could see many parallel characteristics between this Man and the ancient descriptions of the Messiah. I was not sure that I could readily endorse His Messianic tendencies but still I was intrigued and captured by His ministry. As a reasonable man and a natural skeptic when it came to matters of traveling prophets, I had decided to remain aloof and detached from this Man and His ministry. But something completely out of my control quickly changed that stance.

My wife and I had noticed for several months a slow hideous decline in the health of our twelve year old daughter. For many, having a daughter was not considered a reason for great joy, but I was not one of them. My daughter was a source of great pride and joy for me and our family! Her beauty and vivacious spirit were a constant encouragement to both my wife and me. She was a great help to her mother and even at her young age proved to have a strong love for the synagogue, the law, and generally the things of God, which gave me such continued hope.

As I watched her grow tired and frail from week to week, I could not concentrate well on my religious duties. All I could think about was her weakening condition and our inability to do anything to prevent its ravaging effects. Hoping and praying continually for her condition to change, I was reluctant to approach this Jesus, although I knew where He lived and how He spent His time traveling in and out of the city to minister to the crowds of people who followed Him.

I remember that fateful day well! The morning sunrise had not brought its glow to our home. Although it moved upward in the sky, and warmed the whole of the country side, my daughter's condition that morning had declined to such an extent that nothing but gloom seemed to hang in the air throughout our home. By all reports and examinations, my precious daughter was now stepping slowly toward death's door.

It was this final fear and shock that brought me to a change of mind. I must seek out this Jesus of Nazareth! It did not matter whether or not I believed Him to be the Messiah, now; I had no other alternative but to seek this Man for His ability to heal my daughter. I would ignore the mocking thoughts in my mind that wanted me to honor my leadership position, and prestigious place in Judaism, above my desperate need of this miracle worker. In humility and extreme anxiety I would find Him!

Stepping through my front entryway out into the brightness of the day, I wondered where I should look first for this Jesus. After crossing the small courtyard that opened to the road in front of my home, the answer was obvious; I would simply follow the crowd! Looking up and down the small dirty and rocky pathway, I knew I could simply follow the press of people toward the market place, and there I would find this Jesus. Hundreds of people were already on their way to find Him and no doubt planned on getting as close as was possible to Him, in hopes of a miracle.

I quickly joined the movement. The momentum of the people carried me along toward the market place. As I could, I moved around and through groups of people in order to make the most of my time, which was of the essence, now that my daughter was actually dying! I needed to find Him soon! I could not afford a delay or an interruption! He had to be close by or all hope was gone! I pressed forward offering silent prayers to the Lord Jehovah, asking for mercy and help in my greatest time of need!

Suddenly, there in front of me Jesus of Nazareth came into view! Surrounded by people and disciples He was reaching in every direction attempting to touch as many as He could with one hand, while gathering children and the elderly with the other hand, and softly speaking to them. As this flurry of ministry was taking place before me, I could not control my desperation any longer. I forced my way past one last person, and now, standing eye to eye with this hoped for Messiah, I gazed full in His face and then fell in one exhausted pile of human need, begging Him to come to my home, 'My little daughter is at death's door', I cried loudly, 'Come and lay Your hands on her so she can get well and live.' I attempted to say through my tears. To my utter relief and startled joy, this Jesus stopped in His tracks and immediately looked down into my face, still streaked with moisture from a thousand tears, and motioned for me to rise and take the lead and He would follow. Stumbling to my feet I made a quick about face and proceeded back from where I had come, back to the death bed where I had left my daughter earlier in the day. Now, however, I stepped with hope and urgency determined to bring this Jesus to her side.

The crowd did not dissipate in any sense of the word. Everyone simply changed direction and continued following the both of us back toward the synagogue and my home. I continued to offer prayers and pleas for mercy under my breath as we progressed back along the road. Jesus had responded to my plea; now, I only hoped we could make it in time for Him to touch her and restore her strength. In my mind any delay would be costly and tragic in its results, so I rushed forward pushing aside those who seemed to be moving too slowly for my comfort.

It was during this rush forward that for a few brief minutes my world teetered on its edge, threatening to crash down around me! Along the way, back through the market place, Jesus had stopped! Turning to see what had caused His delay, I watched as he looked earnestly, searching through the crowd, asking why someone had touched His garment. What kind of request was that I had thought to myself? I was sure many people had touched Him as He moved through the packed passage ways and streets. Why was that so unusual? And why did He need to stop and clarify the episode! In my amazement and disappointment, I watched as an older woman in the crowd came crawling into the open, and fell at his feet, confessing her need and her previously decided plan to grab His garment. It was here at this point, in their muffled conversation, that I lost all sense of sight and sound.

Unbeknownst to me, as I was plowing my way through the crowd to bring this Jesus home with me, my servants had dispatched a courier, from my home, to find me and report the heartbreaking news that my daughter had died. The courier had made his way, from my house, through the gathering people toward the market place and I had left the market place making my way toward my home. We had met each other at the precise moment that this woman was confessing her situation to Jesus. As the crushing words left the courier's mouth and landed heavy on my ears, I reeled with grief and shock like some invisible club had pounded into my chest! We had been too late! My daughter was now dead!

Attempting to be polite and comforting at the same time, my trusted courier leaned against my shoulder, and attempted to speak only to me, saying simply, 'Your daughter is dead. Why bother the Teacher anymore?' I stood in shocked stiffness for a few brief seconds. Not wanting to accept the words given to me, but realizing that now my request would only be a distraction to this Teacher and Prophet, I had to accept that time had run out and not even this Jesus could change the course of events now. Having no desire to move, not being able to talk because of the exploding sorrow that now coursed in my veins, I seemed to be trapped in my horror; unmovable.

If I had not been interrupted in my grief by an unfamiliar, yet comforting voice, I could have easily remained lost in my darkness for some time, but the strength of this comforting voice pulled me back to reality. 'Don't be afraid. Only believe.' The Teacher was saying to me in front of everyone. And to support His words of hope and expectancy, He had now moved ahead of me on the roadway, and was beckoning me toward my own house! Finding just enough energy to clear my head and put my disillusionment behind me for an instant, I immediately turned to follow.

Pressing forward with steely determination, this Jesus now passed through hundreds of people, stopping this time for no one. Walking directly behind the Master and His core of disciples, I could see along the way that he was talking and making decisive hand motions to His disciples in preparation for His arrival at my home. Not knowing what He meant by these hand motions, nor really caring, I just pressed forward to stay as close as I could to the forward progress of this miracle Man.

Slowly but deliberately along the road as we walked, several of the disciples that followed closely to Jesus began disbursing the press of people. Some were sent home, others were asked to stay behind, and still others were forcibly turned aside and told reassuringly that the Master would continue His ministry later in the day, and at daybreak the following day. By the time we reached the point where the front entryway of my home was visible to our group, only Jesus, three of his key disciples, and me were left to enter the residence. Again I was not sure of the reasoning behind this reduction in personnel but with only one thing on my mind I did not pay very close attention to any logic behind the actions.

Stepping through the open door from the front courtyard, we were met with a commotion and turmoil of weeping and wailing! Voices pierced through the air from every direction as my family and friends did the only thing that seemed natural at the time; they cried aloud, wailing their grief and sorrow. Hearing this sound overwhelmed my emotions and I fought valiantly to not join in their din of lamenting. Jesus was much more straightforward in His reaction. He stepped into the confusion and bluntly asked, 'Why are you making such a commotion and weeping?' which only quieted the sounds of the voices, not their concern. Then without a single thought of hesitation He stated emphatically, 'The child is not dead but asleep.'

This was more than the people could handle. They had come to assist in the grieving process and by joining in with the shedding of tears they were trying to comfort the grieving family. Even if they had not been privy to the details of my daughter's illness, once they were here and had caught a glimpse of her dead lifeless body, their sorrow and tears would have been genuinely expressed.

Now, this stranger, whom many did not recognize, had broken into their sacred custom and spoken like a mad man! What did He mean she was only asleep? He had not even taken the time to view the body and yet He had the gall to announce that she was not dead but only sleeping? This was not just offensive; it was comical to those who heard such lunacy! Before I could calm the situation and offer any explanation for the appearance of this Jesus of Nazareth, many in the room began to laugh. Laughing and mocking at

His words, they raised their voices to resume the previous commotion but this time to demean the very One whom I had asked to come.

What happened next was a surprise to all of us especially those who were still laughing! Jesus made no effort to rebuke or argue with the mockers He simply started motioning everyone to leave. In fact, as many would prove to be too slow in responding to His request, He started escorting them to the door! One by one the room was emptied of its mockers leaving only the six of us; Jesus, His three disciples, me and my wife. I was now intent on watching His actions and His progress. It was clear that He had not come to grieve but take action and I wanted to be the first to see the results. Now, reaching out His hand, He took hold of mine with one of His and with the other hand He took hold of my wife's still trembling hand. Stepping backward several times through the outer living area He led us and His disciples into the small room at the back of the house where I had left my daughter many hours before.

There on the small bed near the side wall of the room laid my lovely child. Serenely she lay in the stillness of death. Peaceful but lifeless! As the scene took shape before me, it took all the inner resolve I could gather to stay focused on the teacher and not on the foreboding grayness of the moment. My wife held tightly to my upper arm, leaned her soft cheek on my sleeve and staring blankly at the empty shell that was once our daughter, cried silently. The disciples of Jesus stood a few steps behind us watching intently the face of the Teacher as if to read some message or signal in His features. As we all looked to the lifeless body on the mat and then to the determined eyes of this miracle worker, we watched as Jesus stepped to the edge of the bed. Bending slightly downward over my daughter's face and reaching to her side, He carefully slipped His fingers under the fingers of her right hand, softly squeezed her dainty and small hand and spoke, 'Little girl, I say to you, get up!'

As the words left this Man's mouth and fell upon my daughter's ears, she immediately quivered and flinched. Beautiful rosy color slowly flushed into her face and neck chasing away the pale colorless look of death. She opened her dark striking eyes toward the ceiling and began to focus them! Slowly, realizing where she was, she turned her head and eyes to meet those of my wife's and my own. A broad smile quickly curved across her lips as she saw us and the Teacher standing over her.

The smile had no more broadened enough to show a peek of her white teeth but she sat up straight, leaned and rolled over to the floor, and with one sudden brace of her hand was standing upright and walking in small circles in the room! All of us burst into shouts of glee and laughter; my wife and I hugging our daughter tightly with tears of joy washing our faces and the three disciples behind us shaking their hands, embracing each other, and offering accompanying expressions of praise and thanksgiving. Jesus the Teacher, Prophet, Messiah and miracle worker stood silently on the side with a gentle smile on His own face as He watched our jubilant hugs, dances and jumps for joy.

We were celebrating our daughter's restored life and could not wait to tell the others who waited faithlessly outside our front doors. As if knowing already our plans, Jesus made a different request. He gave us strict orders to tell no one what had happened and then as a matter of practicality told us to be sure to give our hungry child something to eat. With that He beckoned to His three disciple companions and left.

We on the other hand did not have to tell anyone what had happened, for as soon as my daughter stepped into the rays of the late afternoon sun, the entire group of family and friends who had been previously put out only moments before, now, surrounded her and overwhelmed her with embraces, kisses and of course scores of questions and inquiries. Although we had sworn to be silent, those who now surrounded my daughter had not! And so it wasn't long before the truth was spreading everywhere in the region!

CHAPTER EIGHTEEN:
THE JORDAN CROSSING
JOSHUA 3-4

Historical background and setting

The year is approximately 1400-1410 B.C. Moses has died and Joshua, his trusted assistant, has been appointed as leader in his place. It is now time for the Israelites to make their crossing over the Jordan River into the promised land of Canaan. Thus, the entire nation is camped on the eastern side of the river at a place that Israel called 'Abel-Shittim'. It is some 10 to 12 miles up the gentle sloping valley from the Jordan River. West of the river lay the City Jericho and the camp site of Gilgal, both of which would be key geographical locations in Israel's conquest of Canaan. At 'Abel-Shittim' God will speak to Joshua and give him a very specific plan to get the nation of Israel across the river. It will be practical and miraculous at the same time and one unnamed priest will describe the whole event from his unique vantage point. Let's join the narrative.

The Story

I am a priest from the tribe of Levi. As a Levite I am a direct descendent of our forefather Levi, the son of Jacob. The bible does not mention me by name; however, it does describe my participation in a miraculous crossing of the river Jordan by my people Israel as we began our conquest of the Promised Land. Being called upon to help lead the masses of God's people through the waters of the Jordan was a great privilege; I just had no idea how dramatic it would be in its final expression. This is my story.

As a member of Israel's Levitical priesthood I was assigned the duties of maintaining and caring for the Tabernacle of Moses in the wilderness, with all of its unique and specific furniture and trappings. On a regularly basis during our travels from Egypt to the Jordan shores, I had helped set up the great Tabernacle and assisted the people of Israel in their daily and weekly sacrificial requirements. This Tabernacle with its outer court and holy inner chambers was central to our formal worship of Jehovah! Almost daily I was exposed to the glorious sight of God's Shekinah glory leading his people. During the daylight hours, whether traveling or camping, the great mass of several million people were led by the dictates of the billowing churning cloud of God's presence, which paved the way through the parched and treacherous Wilderness of Sin. At night, with the dark surroundings of a foreboding desert, each of the twelve tribes of Israel would nestle closely around the Tabernacle in restive camping formation and I would stand in awe as the whitish beige cloud of glory transformed itself into a churning boiling pillar of fire! God would literal stand as either a towering smoking pillar or a soaring burning sentinel, offering direct protection for Moses, Joshua and the entire nation of Israel. During those unfortunate years of wandering, I was blessed to have watched this phenomenon many times and it never seemed to be mundane or tiring for me! It was breath taking to say the least each time I was privileged to see it.

Now, after forty years of wilderness wandering and desert crisscrossing, we were perched overlooking the Jordan River valley ready for our final movement into Canaan. Having endured the forty year death march, in which my fathers had died and were buried in the wilderness due to their disobedience to God, made this final encampment a bitter sweet experience. Many of us, as good Israelites, were deeply saddened at the failure of our forefathers to enter the Promised Land but were at the same time exhilarated at the reality of what now lay before us. The final approach to this current location had taken us around the territories of Edom and Moab, since these future neighbors were highly suspicious of us.

From these upper eastern hillsides of the Jordan River valley we began the preparation to invade a hostile but lovely land. Looking to the west we could see the Jordan River snaking its way along in front of us at the very bottom of the valley floor as it flowed from the north to the south. This ancient river, named for its 'decent' from the mountains far to the north of the Sea of Galilee, flowed ever lower in elevation until it emptied into the Dead Sea not too far to the south of our present location. In the far distance beyond the river and up the opposite gentle rise from the valley, the City of Jericho was in clear view with its huge barrier walls refracting light from the sun back toward us. This ominous walled city would eventually be our first point of conflict with the inhabitants of Canaan. Spreading along the low hills like a bristling fluttering fabric piece in the breeze, the twelve tribes of Israel, each with their teeming thousands hugged the ground in anticipation of possessing what they now could see in the distance. Throughout the entire camp a nervous excitement was building each day as we awaited instruction from Joshua about the timing and procedure of our crossing.

Since we had been told to expect the possibility of fierce military resistance on the part of our enemies upon crossing the Jordan, I anticipated watching several of our own warring tribes be assembled in the front of our tribal groupings to lead the initial thrust. This, in my mind, would be needed in an effort to push back any developing resistance from the far side of the valley. I fully expected that after our preparation was concluded, a strong show of weaponry would be brought to the front and placed strategically in full view of our enemies. Our three days of consecration and personal sanctification, while waiting at the water's edge, seemed normal enough for such a monumental entry into our promised land. With the memory of our past disobedience still fresh in our minds, we did not want to enter our future homeland without preparing our hearts and examining our motives as a nation. And certainly we could ill afford to rush in without waiting on God for his leadership in this matter. So imagine my surprise and shock when, after our days of self reflection had ended, rather than warriors, I was called upon to assist in bringing the Ark of God to the front instead!

Carrying the Ark of God was an incredible honor! This piece of furniture was the most important of all the furniture pieces that were associated with the Tabernacle. This piece and this piece alone represented the very presence of Jehovah! And it was the very presence of Jehovah that had marked us a peculiar and unique people. During the many years that the nation of Israel journeyed to this final destination my association with the Ark of God became very familiar. Its golden cherubim, mercy seat, crowned upper edge, golden poles and rings elicited visions of grandeur every time I serviced its needs and helped carry it from camp site to camp site. Many times I would try to imagine its blood stained mercy seat top and the two gold crouching Cherubim being energized by the glowing pulsating energy of the Shekinah. As I would place the two golden poles through the gold metal rings on either side of the box and drape the cover over the angel wings reaching to touch their tips I would dream of how it might look sitting reverently in the Holy of Holies. I would never, of course, be able to view that scene first hand since that was reserved for the High Priest only. But none the less I imagined many times what it might be like to see such majesty.

Now, however, this sacred focal point of God's active presence among his people was to be brought into full view of the entire congregation. This prospect piqued my attention greatly. I wondered if we would see a glimpse of the unspeakable presence from between the golden Cherubim. I had most often seen the Ark while it was in transit but now it would be brought into action for all to see! I wondered if there would be a surge of power from this sacred box that would transform the river somehow, allowing us to cross without danger. Would the cloud or fire appear and set in motion some strange course of events to provide the crossing? The possibilities were intriguing to say the least! Although I knew the mere sight of the Ark would inspire loyalty and courage in the people, I remained puzzled about the instruction we had received to bring the Ark to the river and how it related to our crossing of the water.

Joshua had asked us to bring the Ark of God to the water's edge and wait. He reminded us while we waited, that the people were instructed to watch and follow at a distance of 1000 yards so as not to lose sight of us and the Ark. Several reasons for this strange approach made sense to me as I pondered the instructions. First of all, we were in unfamiliar and uncharted territory, so keeping the Ark in full view insured our common destination; Secondly, the press of people was so large that being too close could jeopardize the priest's ability to safely carry the Ark by jostling our progress; and thirdly, the Jordan River itself was at flood stage making the shoreline unpredictable in its stability and access. So being able to see the Ark of God at all times during this crossing was imperative!

Joining the three others assigned to the Ark I found my place at one of the corners. At a previously arranged moment of command I joined the other three in reaching to each of our poles and hoisting them evenly up to our shoulders. As the poles were lifted upward I could feel the weight of the gold and wood behind me pull against our lifting motion. Slowly we bore the weight of God's earthly throne between us! The Ark of God now hung in mid air from only four gold loops and two gold covered poles while

197

being borne on the shoulders of four stately priests. With careful cadence and coordinated steps, our foursome made its way down the sloped terrain toward the river. People watching moved backwards from us in all directions to give us plenty of room to turn, proceed off of the rockier hillside and find a non-obscured place just off the water's edge. Once to the river, we cautiously but firmly gripped our pole ends with both of our strong hands and wrists and leaning slightly inward toward the Ark itself, lowered the holy box to the ground. I straightened back to my full height and turned slightly away from the Ark and looked back to the eager crowd. All I could see was vast groupings of people spreading up and down the river's edge and back toward the distant hills watching our maneuvers and eagerly waiting for what was to come next. It was odd being the center of attention for hundreds of thousands of God's chosen people.

Joshua now approached the four of us as we stood guard over the Ark of God. His instructions were short and clear. With the entire nation watching, we were to lift the Ark to our shoulders as before and take several steps into the water. At the point that our feet entered the current of the Jordan's water, the Lord God would take action to divide the waters and allow the people to pass over. We were to simply step into the water and stand our ground and God would do the rest! This seemed so unorthodox to my way of thinking. Over the years of my service to the Tabernacle I had been sworn to protect the Ark at all cost and to insure that it was not damaged, mistreated or tarnished during our long months and years of traveling away from Egypt and Sinai. Now, the Ark was being positioned to protect us and insure the safe travel of an entire nation through a flood swollen river into a foreign but Promised Land.

Again each of us at the four corners of the Ark lifted our poles and brought the full weight of its presence and sacred structure to our shoulders. And once more with careful ordering of our steps we paced our strides to bring our holy cargo perpendicular to the river, the Ark and we four priests facing out over the twisting brown water. Then with the eyes of an entire nation fixed upon us we made those first steps into the water.

My first step into the brown swirling water brought a shiver up my leg as the cold stabbed at my sandaled feet. Stepping into the water, while at the same time steadying the Ark was a bit of a challenge, especially with the shock of cold water against our skin, the current pulling at our ankles and the slick rocks under foot threatening to slide at any given moment. But with the finish of our first stride and each of our four final steps leaving us simply standing in several inches of water everything changed! The water under us began to move away from our feet as if to react and retreat from the force of our steps. Moving out from under us like an invisible shock wave, the water's surface began to roll and bubble and spread away from the Ark.

Out in front of us, aiming straight at the shoreline a distinct line was beginning to cut into the top of the curling water like an invisible sword. It was being gradually slicing the moving water! As all of us watched, the cutting action began separating the water coming from the north from the water leaving us to the south. Just off to our right a few yards upstream the water began piling up upon itself, inching further and further backward up the river channel. As if some unseen barrier was being pushed down through the water into the rocky bed below, the downward flow of water was blocked. I stared in amazement as the rivers surface divided, swelling and widening as it was being pushed up the river valley as far as the small city of Adam. Downstream the water was moving away from us as if moving into some huge drain hole beyond our sight. It was draining away and leaving the river bottom completely exposed to the elements and our amazed eyes! Rocks, boulders, mud, pebbles, sand and small disappearing puddles were all that was left as the energy of God's glory seemed to pour out of the Ark of God into the Jordan River bed. We were feeling no particular energy surge or sensation but never the less the invisible strength of God's power was revealing itself for all to see! As the action continued, it became crystal clear as to the mode of crossing we would take. The people of God would again cross a once full watery barrier on dry ground, just as they had done at the Red Sea so many years ago!

As we stood not more than five feet into the river with the Ark again hanging between us, the people began their slow methodical march to the far shore. Giving a wide birth to the Ark and it holy contents, they picked and wove their way through the now drying river bed. While watching their footing in the exposed bottom of the river, serious looks of awe and amazement where projected our way. Almost every person stared toward us standing solemnly at the shoreline. The emotion was no doubt intense as they viewed the Ark; watched us holding its four corners and hearing the water bubbling and roiling beyond us. As well they were seeing the pushed up water holding firm in its eight feet height across the whole of the river's width! God was proving himself strong to a new generation of Israelites and confirming the leadership of Joshua at the same time and the people knew it! The atmosphere was light, festive and teeming with excitement as the great horde of people and animals took their turns passing us and proceeding down into the dry river bed, across its now open expanse, and then up and onto the west side of the valley. As each grouping of people would slowly move into view of our prominent position, the reaction would be the same; first a puzzled questioning look, then a wide-eyed startled realization of what was happening and then smiles, laughter, giddiness and periodic shouts of praise to Jehovah would finish their look toward us. Many would remain with their faces fixed in amazement as they were pushed forward by the momentum of the tightly placed people behind them. They almost stumbling as their stare outlasted their balance and forward progress!

I wondered out loud to my three companion priests that if any of our enemies; the Canaanites, Hittites, Hivites, Perizzites, Girgashites, Amorites, and Jebusites happen to be in the area and were watching this, no doubt the sight was striking a deep panic in their hearts. Here in the heart of Canaan, the people of God who were delivered from Egypt, given the law at Sinai and then...purified through forty years in the desert were NOW being escorted miraculously into the very front yard of the occupying nations. As would be confirmed later this indeed brought great fear upon all who heard of our entry into the land.

We had stood our ground for some time now and finally could see the last of the people moving out of the river bed ahead of us. There was only one final thing to do before we brought the Ark of God across the dry river bottom to the other side. Watching intently now so as not to delay our own crossing, we viewed the last step in the process with anxious eyes. From the other side of the river, one by one, twelve different men came filtering through the people as they milled around the opposite shore line.

These twelve made their way back down to the middle of the empty dry river bed and began sorting and sifting through rocks and boulders which now lay helpless in the sun. Each of the twelve men, one man from each of the twelve tribes of Israel, grunted and wrestled into their grip a large stone. Then each of them lifted to a shoulder and carried back to the far side of the river bed their own stone and stacked it, with the others, closely in a small column-like form. This pile of large river stones would later be made in to a sort of makeshift marker or memorial locator but now it signaled our need to finalize the crossing by our own venture along the dry sandy bottom of the Jordan.

These standing stones would be the subject of conversations for many years into the future as God's people recounted this supernatural crossing to the next generation. After the twelve stones were deposited on the shoreline, to our startled attention, Joshua himself made his way out to meet us in the middle of the river bed and quickly arranged twelve stones of his own just to the side of where we stood with the Ark. Now the once impassable, but opened water barrier would be marked as well with a memorial to God's work!

Insuring that we walked in complimentary rhythm, we made our way along the same path that our people had traveled ahead of us. Passing the center of the river bed I could see the large gaping holes where the locator stones had been pried loose and removed. Leaving the twelve stones of Joshua and these temporary muddy markers at our back, we slowly moved toward the river's edge. It was then that the voice of Joshua echoed over our heads, 'Come up from the Jordan', he called to us as we made our way toward him. Making our way some ten to twelve feet up on the rocky shoreline, we again carefully lowered the Ark of God temporarily to the ground and quickly turned to view the expanse of rock, mud and stone we had just exited. With no more than the time it took us to turn our heads, the waters of the Jordan began crashing and flushing forward back into the void of the empty river bed. As if some hidden hand had yanked the barrier from in front of the piled up water, from the west shore back to the east shore, the weight of the pent up water surged down splashing, splattering, foaming and rushing back to it former place between its containing banks. The mighty Jordan River was again flowing to it final destination in the Dead Sea.

Now, for the four of us who were charged with the care of the Ark of God, we hoisted the sacred box back to our shoulders and carried it along to the camping area at Gilgal. The whole nation would remain camping here for several days to finish preparations for the initial conquest of Canaan. We had now become officially cut off from our past wonderings and the previous disobedience of our forefathers. This camp site at Gilgal would prove to be a crucial way station into the Promised Land as new male circumcision, battle preparation and spying out the City of Jericho would dominate our energy and attention for several days. For now, the Ark was to be carried back to the Levitical camp. It would be covered and returned to its resting place among the Tabernacle trimmings and furniture, but without a full construction of the worship center. We had entered a new era and a new way of thinking would now mark our worship and dedication to Jehovah.

Making our way gingerly through the scattered and busy people, we passed the central gathering area and once again saw the twelve neatly piled stones from the river. They had been strategically placed in this high traffic area for all the tribes of Israel to see as they came and went setting up camp for our stay at Gilgal. Feeling the heavy but gentle sway of the Ark as it hung between us, I rehearsed in my mind Joshua's last words given to us as we turned our attention away from the river just a few hours previously. He had made sure that we knew the significance of these twelve stones and their placement. They had been set up as a memorial to the work of God at the Jordan! We were to mark the meaning of their placement and their location in our minds so our children could hear us rehearse the events of this glorious day. In the future, when our children asked us about the meaning of these stones, we could then explain in detail how the LORD God had dried up the waters of the Jordan allowing us to cross on dry ground just as He had done to the Red Sea so many year ago. This and the previous, miraculous crossing were intended to make an indelible impression upon all of the people of Israel and invoke a healthy fear of the Lord in their hearts. And that they did! But also the dividing of these waters was intended as a statement of intention on the part of God, so that all the people of the earth would know that the LORD intended to defend his people Israel and his hand is mighty to save!

The End

DOUGLAS S. MALOTT

Author Biography

Douglas S. Malott currently resides in Spokane, Washington with wife, Patti, where he was born and raised. Doug and Patti have been married for 35 years and have 4 grown children and one really great son-in-law, along with the cutest grandson ever! Doug has been in the ministry since 1980 and has been the Senior Pastor at The Rock of Ages Christian Fellowship since 1982. Pastor Malott has his Bachelors' Degree in Business and Education from Whitworth University, in Spokane Washington, and his Masters Degree in Biblical Studies from Trinity College of the Bible and Seminary in Newburgh, Indiana.

Made in the USA
Las Vegas, NV
07 September 2022

54843292R00118